LIKES

LIKES

SARAH
SHUN-LIEN
BYNUM

FARRAR, STRAUS AND GIROUX

NEW YORK

Farrar, Straus and Giroux
120 Broadway, New York 10271

Grateful acknowledgment is made to the publications in which some
of these stories originally appeared, in slightly different form: *Tin House*
("The Young Wife's Tale"); *Ploughshares* ("Tell Me My Name" and "Julia and
Sunny"); *The New Yorker* ("The Erlking," "Many a Little Makes," "The
Burglar," "Likes," and "Bedtime Story"); and *Glimmer Train* ("The Bears").

Library of Congress Cataloging-in-Publication Data
Names: Bynum, Sarah Shun-lien, author.
Title: Likes / Sarah Shun-lien Bynum.
Description: First edition. | New York : Farrar, Straus and Giroux, 2020.
Identifiers: LCCN 2020012454 | ISBN 9780374191948 (hardcover)
Classification: LCC PS3602.Y58 A6 2020 | DDC 813/.6—dc23
LC record available at https://lccn.loc.gov/2020012454

Designed by Gretchen Achilles

Our books may be purchased in bulk for promotional, educational, or
business use. Please contact your local bookseller or the Macmillan Corporate
and Premium Sales Department at 1-800-221-7945, extension 5442, or by
e-mail at MacmillanSpecialMarkets@macmillan.com.

www.fsgbooks.com
www.twitter.com/fsgbooks • www.facebook.com/fsgbooks

1 3 5 7 9 10 8 6 4 2

For Willa

CONTENTS

THE ERLKING   3

TELL ME MY NAME   19

THE YOUNG WIFE'S TALE   41

THE BEARS   60

MANY A LITTLE MAKES   81

THE BURGLAR   124

JULIA AND SUNNY   151

LIKES   179

BEDTIME STORY   202

LIKES

THE ERLKING

It is just as Kate hoped. The worn path, the bells tinkling on the gate. The huge fir trees dropping their needles one by one. A sweet mushroomy smell, gnomes stationed in the underbrush, the sound of a mandolin far up on the hill. "We're here, we're here," she says to her child, who isn't walking fast enough and needs to be pulled along by the hand. Through the gate they go, up the dappled path, beneath the firs, across the school parking lot and past the kettle-corn stand, into the heart of the Elves' Faire.

Her child is named Ondine but answers only to Ruthie. Ruthie's hand rests damply in hers, and together they watch two scrappy fairies race by, the swifter one waving a long string of raffle tickets. "Don't you want to wear your wings?" Kate asked that morning, but Ruthie wasn't in the mood. Sometimes they are in cahoots, sometimes not. Now they circle the great shady lawn, studying the activities. There is candle making, beekeeping, the weaving of God's eyes. A sign in purple calligraphy says that King

Arthur will be appearing at noon. There's a tea garden, a bluegrass band, a man with a thin sandy beard and a hundred acorns pinned with bright ribbons to the folds of his tunic, boys thumping one another with jousting sticks. The ground is scattered with pine needles and hay. The lemonade cups are compostable. Everything is exactly as it should be, every small elvish detail attended to, but, as Kate's heart fills with the pleasure of it all, she is made uneasy by the realization that she could have but did not secure this for her child, and therein lies a misjudgment, a possibly grave mistake.

They had not even applied to a Waldorf school! Kate's associations at the time were vague but nervous-making: devil sticks, recorder playing, occasional illiteracy. She thought she remembered hearing about a boy who, at nine, could map the entire Mongol empire but was still sucking his fingers. That couldn't be good. Everybody has to go into a 7-Eleven at some point in life, operate in the ordinary universe. So she didn't even sign up for a tour. But no one ever told her about the whole fairy component. And now look at what Ruthie is missing. Magic. Nature. Flower wreaths, floating playsilks, an unpolluted, media-free experience of the world. The chance to spend her days binding books and acting out stories with wonderful wooden animals made in Germany.

Ruthie wants to take one home with her, a baby giraffe. Mysteriously, they have ended up in the sole spot at the Elves' Faire where commerce occurs and credit cards are accepted. Ruthie is not even looking at the baby giraffe;

with some nonchalance, she keeps it tucked under her arm as she touches all the other animals on the table.

"A macaw!" she cries softly to herself, reaching.

Kate finds a second baby giraffe, caught between a buffalo and a penguin. Although the creatures represent a wide range of the animal kingdom, they all appear to belong to the same dear, blunt-nosed family. The little giraffe is light in her hand, but when she turns it over to read the tiny price tag stuck to the bottom of its feet she puts it down immediately. Seventeen dollars! Enough to feed an entire fairy family for a month. Noah's Ark, looming in the middle of the table, now looks somewhat sinister. Two by two, two by two. It adds up.

How do the Waldorf parents manage? How do any parents manage? Kate hands over her Visa.

She says to Ruthie, "This is a very special thing. Your one special thing from the Elves' Faire, okay?"

"Okay," Ruthie says, looking for the first time at the animal that is now hers. She knows that her mother likes giraffes; at the zoo, she stands for five or ten minutes at the edge of the giraffe area, talking about their beautiful large eyes and their long lovely eyelashes. She picked the baby giraffe for her mother because it's her favorite. Also because she knew that her mother would say yes, and she does not always say yes—for instance, when asked about My Little Pony. So Ruthie was being clever but also being kind. She was thinking of her mother while also thinking of herself. Besides, there are no My Little Ponies to be found at this fair—she's looked. But a baby giraffe will need a mother to go with it. There is a bigger giraffe on the table, and maybe in five minutes Ruthie will ask if she can put it on her birthday list.

"Mommy," Ruthie says, "is my birthday before Christmas or after?"

"Well, it depends what you mean by before," Kate says unhelpfully.

Holding hands, they leave the elves' marketplace and climb up the sloping lawn to the heavy old house at the top of the hill, with its low-pitched roof and stout columns and green-painted eaves. Kate guesses that this whole place was once the fresh-air retreat of a tubercular rich person, but now it's a center of child-initiated learning.

Ruthie's own school is housed in a flat prefab trailer-type structure tucked behind the large parking lot of a Korean church. It's lovely in its way, with a mass of morning-glory vines softening things up, and, in lieu of actual trees, a mural of woodland scenes painted along the outside wall. And parking is never a problem, which is a plus, since at other schools that can be a real issue at dropoff and pickup. At Wishing Well, the parents take turns wearing reflective vests and carrying walkie-talkies, just to manage the morning traffic inching along the school's driveway. Or there's the grim Goodbye Door at the Jewish Montessori, beyond the threshold of which the dropping-off parent is forbidden to pass. For philosophical reasons, of course, but anyone who's seen the line of cars double-parked outside the building on a weekday morning might suppose a more practical agenda—namely, limited street parking does not allow for long farewells. To think that the Jewish Montessori was once the school Kate had set her heart on! She wouldn't have survived that awful departure, the sound of her own weeping as she turned off her emergency blinkers and made her slow way down the street.

But she had been enchanted by the Jewish Montessori, helplessly enchanted, not even minding (truth be told) the ghastly tales of the Door. Instantly she had loved the vaulted ceiling and the skylights, the Frida Kahlo prints hanging on the walls, the dainty Shabbat candlesticks, and the feeling of coolness and order that was everywhere. On the day of her visit, she'd sat on a little canvas folding stool and watched in wonder as the children silently unfurled their small rugs around the room and then settled into their private, absorbing, intricate tasks. She'd felt her heart begin to slow, felt the relief of finally pressing the mute button on a chortling TV. How clearly she saw that she needn't have been burdened for all these years with her own harried and inefficient self, that her thoughts could have been more elegant, her neural pathways less congested—if only her parents had chosen differently for her. If only they had given her this!

But the school had not made the least impression on Ondine. Every Saturday morning for ten weeks, the two of them had shuffled up the steps with eighteen other applicants and undergone a lengthy, rigorous audition process disguised as a Mommy & Me class. Kate would break out in a light sweat straightaway. Ondine would show only occasional interest in spooning lima beans from a small wooden bowl to a slightly larger one. "Remember, that's *his* job," Kate would whisper urgently as Ondine made a grab for another kid's eyedropper. The parents were supposed to preserve the integrity of each child's work space, and all these odd little projects—the beans, the soap shavings, the tongs and the muffin tin, even the puzzles—were supposed to be referred to as jobs.

Ten weeks of curious labor, and then the rejection letter arrived, on rainbow stationery. Kate was such an idiot—she sat right down and wrote a thank-you note to the school's intimidating and faintly glamorous director in the hope of improving Ondine's chances for the following year. Maybe a few more spots for brown girls would open up? She had never been so crushed. "You're not even Jewish," her mother said, not a little uncharitably. Her friend Hilary, a Montessori Mommy & Me dropout, confessed to feeling kind of relieved on her behalf. "Didn't it seem, you know, a bit robotic? Or maybe Dickensian? Like children in a boot-blacking factory." She reminded Kate about the director's car, which they had seen parked one Saturday morning in its specially reserved spot. "Aren't you glad you won't be paying for the plum-colored Porsche?"

Kate wasn't glad. And she did take it personally, despite everybody's advice not to. Week after week, she and her child had submitted themselves to the director's appraising, professional eye, and, for all their earnest effort, they had still been found wanting. What flaw or lack did she see in them that they couldn't yet see in themselves? Even though

Kate spoke about the experience in a jokey, self-mocking way, she could tell that it made people uncomfortable to hear her ask this question, and she learned to do so silently, when she was driving around the city by herself or with Ondine asleep in the back of the car.

"Can I get the mommy giraffe for Christmas?" Ruthie asks at the end of what she estimates is five minutes. She stops at the bottom of the steps leading up to the big green house and waits for an answer. She wants an answer, but she also wants to practice ballet dancing, so she takes many quick tiny steps back and forth, back and forth, like a *Nutcracker* snowflake in toe shoes.

"People are trying to come down the stairs," her mother says. "Do you have to go potty? Let's go find the potty."

"I'm just dancing!" Ruthie says. "You're hurting my feelings."

"You have to go potty," her mother says. "I can tell. And Daddy told you: no more accidents." But Ruthie sees that she is not really concentrating—she is looking at the big map of the Elves' Faire and finding something interesting—and Ruthie will hold the jiggly snowflake feeling inside her body for as long as she wants. This will mean that she wins, because when she doesn't go potty regular things like walking or standing are more exciting. She's having an adventure.

"It says there's a doll room. Does that sound fun? A special room filled with fairy dolls." Her mother leans closer to the map and then looks around at the real place, trying to make them match. "I think it's down there." She points with the hand that is not holding Ruthie's.

Ruthie wants to see what her mother is pointing at, but instead she sees a man. He is standing at the bottom of the hill and looking up at her. He is not the acorn man, and he does not have a golden crown like the kind a king wears, or the pointy hat of a wizard. She has seen Father Christmas by the raffle booth, and this is not him. This is not a father or a teacher or a neighbor. He does not smile like the brown man who sells popsicles from a cart. This man is tall and thin, with a cape around his neck that is not black or blue but a color in between, a middle-of-the-night color, and he pushes back the hood on his head and looks at her as if he knows her.

"Do you see where I'm pointing?" Kate asks, and suddenly squats down and peers into Ruthie's face. Sometimes there's a bit of a lag, she's noticed, a disturbing faraway look. It could be lack of sleep: The consistent early bedtime that Dr. Weissbluth strongly recommends just hasn't happened for them yet. A simple enough thing when you read about it, but the reality! Every evening the clock keeps ticking—through dinner, dessert, bath, books, the last unwilling whizz of the day—and, with all the various diversions and spills and skirmishes, Kate wonders if it would be easier to disarm a bomb in the time allotted. And so Ruthie is often tired. Which could very well explain the slowness to respond; the intractability; the scary, humiliating fits. Maybe even the intensified hair-twirling? It's equally possible that Kate is just fooling herself, and something is actually wrong.

Tonight she'll do a little research on the internet.

Slowly, Kate stands up and tugs at Ruthie's hand. They are heading back down the hill in search of the doll room. They are having a special day, just the two of them. They both like the feeling of being attached by the hand but with their thoughts branching off in different directions. It is similar to the feeling of falling asleep side by side, which they do sometimes, in defiance of Dr. Weissbluth's guidelines, their bodies touching and their dreams going someplace separate but connected. They both like the feeling of not knowing who is leading, whether it's the grown-up or the child.

But Ruthie knows that neither of them is the leader right now. The man wearing the cape is the leader, and he wants them to come to the bottom of the hill. She can tell by the way he's looking at her—kind, but also as if he could get a little angry. They have to come quickly. Spit-spot! No getting distracted. These are the rules. They walk down the big lawn, past the face-painting table and some jugglers and the honeybees dancing behind glass, and Ruthie sees on the man's face that her mother doesn't really have to come at all. Just her.

She has a sneaky feeling that the man is holding a present under his cape. It's supposed to be a surprise. A surprise that is small and very delicate, like a music box, but when you open it, it goes down and down, like a rabbit hole, and inside there is everything—everything—she has wanted: stickers, jewels, books, dolls, high heels, pets, ribbons, purses, toe shoes, makeup. You can't even begin to count! Part of the present is that she doesn't have to choose. So many special and beautiful things, and she wants all of them—she will have all of them—and gone is the crazy feeling she gets when she's in Target and needs the Barbie Island Princess Styling Head so badly that she thinks she's going to throw up. That's the sort of surprise it is. The man is holding a present for her, and when she opens it she will be the kindest, luckiest person in the world. Also the prettiest. Not for pretend—for real life. The man is a friend of her parents, and he has brought a present for her the way her parents' friends from New York or Canada sometimes do. She wants him to be like that, she wants him to be someone who looks familiar. She asks, "Mommy, do we know that man?" and her mother says, "The man with the guitar on his back?" But she's wrong, she's ruined it: he doesn't even have a guitar.

Ruthie doesn't see who her mother is talking about, or why her voice has got very quiet. "Oh wow," her mother whispers. "That's John C. Reilly. How funny. His kids must go here." Then she sighs and says, "I bet they do." She looks at Ruthie strangely. "You know who John C. Reilly is?"

"Who's John C. Reilly?" Ruthie asks, but only a small part of her is talking to her mother; the rest of her is thinking about the surprise. The man has turned his head away, and she can see only the nighttime color of his cape. She sees that there is something moving around underneath his cape, like a little mouse crawling all over his shoulders and trying to get out. She is worried that he might not give the present to her anymore. She is sure that her mother has ruined it.

"Just a person who's in movies. Grown-up movies." Kate's favorite is the one where he plays the tall, sad policeman; he was so lovable in that. Talking to himself, driving around all day in the rain. You just wanted to hand him a towel and give him a hug. And though something about that movie was off—the black woman handcuffed, obese and screaming, and how the boy had to offer up a solemn little rap—John C. Reilly was not himself at fault. He was just doing his job. Playing the part. Even those squirmy scenes were shot through with his goodness. His homely radiance! The bumpy overhang of his brow. His big head packed full of good thoughts and goofy jokes. Imagine sitting next to him on a parents' committee, or at Back-to-School Night! She'd missed her chance. Now he and his guitar are disappearing into the fir trees beyond the parking lot.

Kate sighs. "Daddy and I respect him a lot. He makes really interesting choices."

"Mommy!" Ruthie cries. "Stop talking. Stop talking!" She pulls her hand away and crosses her arms over her chest. "I'm so mad at you right now."

Because another girl, not her, is going to get the surprise. The man isn't even looking at her anymore. He liked her so much before, but he's changed his mind. Her mother didn't see him—she saw only who she wanted to see—and now everything is so damaged and ruined. It's not going to work. "You're making me really angry," Ruthie tells her. "You did it on purpose! I'm going to kick you." She shows her teeth.

"What did I do now?" her mother asks. "What just happened?" She is asking an imaginary friend who's a grown-up standing next to her, not Ruthie. She has nothing to say to Ruthie; she grabs her wrist and marches fast down the hill, trying to get them away from something, from Ruthie's bad mood, probably, and Ruthie is about to cry, because she is not having a good day, her wrist is stinging very badly, nothing is going her way, but just as her mother is dragging her through the door of a small barn she sees again the man with the surprise. He has turned back to look at her, so much closer now, and when he reaches out to touch her she sees that he has long, yellowish fingernails and, under his cape, he's made out of straw. He nods at her slowly. It's going to be okay.

Inside the barn, Kate takes a breath. It actually worked. Nothing like a little force and velocity! Ruthie has been yanked out from under whatever dark cloud she conjured up. Kate will have to try that again. The doll room, strung with Christmas lights, twinkles around her merrily. Bits of tulle and fuzzy yarn hang mistily from the rafters. As her eyes get used to the dim barn and its glimmering light, she sees that there are dolls everywhere, of all possible sizes, perched on nests of leaves and swinging from birch branches and asleep in polished walnut-shell cradles. Like the wooden animals, they seem all to be descended from the same bland and adorable ancestor, a wide-eyed, thin-lipped soul with barely any nose and a mane of bouclé hair. They are darling, irresistible; she wants to squeeze every last one of them and stroke the neat felt shoes on their feet. Little cardboard tags dangle from their wrists or ankles, bearing the names of their makers, faithful and nimble-fingered Waldorf mothers who can also, it's rumored, spin wool! On real wooden spinning wheels. What a magical, soothing, practical skill. Could that be what she lacks—a spinning wheel? She glances down at Ruthie—is she charmed? happy?—and then looks anxiously around the room at the sweet assortment of milky faces peeking out from under tiny elf caps or heaps of luxuriant hair. Please let there be some brown dolls! she thinks. And please let them be cute. Wearing gauzy, sparkly fairy outfits like the others, and not overalls or bonnets or dresses made of calico. A brown mermaid would be nice for once. A brown Ondine. She squeezes her daughter's hand in helpless apology, for even at the Elves' Faire, where all is enchanting and mindful and biodegradable, Kate is again exposing her to something toxic.

But Ruthie isn't even looking at the dolls, because now she has to pee very badly. Also, she can't find her giraffe. It isn't there under her arm, where she left it. Her baby giraffe! It must have slipped out somewhere. But where? There are many, many places it could be. Ruthie looks down at the floor of the barn, which is covered in bits of straw. Not here. She feels her stomach begin to hurt. It was her one special thing from the Elves' Faire. A present from her mother. Maybe her last present from her mother, who might say, *If you can't take care of your special things, then I won't be able to get you special things anymore.* But she won't need special things anymore! She is going to get a surprise, one that gets bigger and bigger the more she thinks about it, because she has a feeling the man is able to do things her mother is not able to do, like let her live in a castle that is also a farm, where she can live in a beautiful tower and have a little kitten and build it a house and give it toys. Also she's going to have five—no, she means ten—pet butterflies.

The man is standing outside the barn now, waiting for her, and maybe if she doesn't come out soon he'll walk right in and get her. Ruthie wants to run and scream; she can't tell if she's happy or the most scared she's ever been. "Noooooooo!" she shrieks when her father holds her upside down and tickles her, but as soon as he stops she cries, "Again, again!" She always wants more of this, and her father and mother always stop too soon.

The man in the cape won't stop. The dolls in this room are children, children he has turned into dolls. Ruthie can help him—she'll be on his team. She'll tell the children, *I'm going to put you in jail. Lock, lock! You're in jail. And I have the key. You can never get out until I tell you.* Her friends from school, her ballet teacher Miss Sara, her best friends Lark and Chloe, her gymnastics coach Tanya, her mommy and daddy, her favorite, specialest people, all sitting with their legs straight out and their eyes wide open, and no one can see them but her. She will be on the stage copying Dorothy, and they will be watching. She will do the whole *Wizard of Oz* for them from the beginning, and the man will paint her skin so it's bright, not brown, and make her hair smooth and in braids so she looks like the real Dorothy. It will be the big surprise of their life!

Kate knows there must be a brown doll somewhere in this barn, and that it's possibly perfect. If anyone can make the doll she's been looking for, these Waldorf mothers can: something touchable and dreamy, something she can give her child to cherish, something her child will love and prefer, instead of settle for. Considering that she's been searching for this doll since the moment Ondine was born, a hundred and thirty dollars is not so much to spend. For every doll in this barn can be purchased, she's just discovered; on the back of each little cardboard tag is a penciled number, and it's become interesting to compare the numbers and wonder why this redheaded doll in a polka-dot dress is twenty-five dollars more than the one wearing a cherry-print apron. She wanders farther into the barn, glancing at the names and numbers, idly doing arithmetic in her head: how much this day has cost so far (seventeen for the giraffe, eight for the smoothies, two for raffle tickets) and how much it might end up costing in the future. Because, if she does find the doll she's looking for, it'd be wonderful to get that white shelf she's been thinking about, a white shelf that she could buy at Ikea for much less than a similar version at Pottery Barn Kids, and nearly as nice, a shelf she could hang in a cheerful spot in Ondine's yellow room from which the doll would then gaze down at her daughter with its benign embroidered eyes and cast a spell of protection. All told, with the doll and the giraffe and the smoothies and the shelf, this day could come in at close to two hundred dollars, but who would blink at that? She's thinking about her child.

Your attention, please! Ruthie will say. *Ladies and gentlemen, your attention! Welcome to the show!* And the man with the cape will pull back the curtains and everybody will be so surprised by what they see that they will put their hands over their mouths and scream.

But Ruthie's own surprise is already turning into something else, not a beautiful secret anymore but just a thing that she knows will happen, whether she wants it to or not, just as she knows that she will have an accident in the barn and her giraffe will be lost and her mother will keep looking at the tags hanging from the dolls' feet, looking closely like she's reading an important announcement, looking closely and not seeing the puddle getting bigger on the floor. When it happens, her mother will be holding her hand—she is always holding and pulling and squeezing her hand—which is impossible, actually, because Ruthie, clever girl, kind girl, ballet dancer, hair-twirler, brave and bright Dorothy, is already gone.

TELL ME MY NAME

Ever since the California economy collapsed, people have been coming to our street at night and going through the trash. That sounds worse than it is—I guess if it's recyclable then it's not really trash. They sort through the blue bins that during the day were wheeled out to the curb, along with the black and green bins, by the gardening crews. The people who come at night are like a crew too. You used to see just solo collectors but over the past few months they seem to have joined forces. They're efficient, with one of them holding on to the grocery cart and organizing things while the others pull out bottles from the bins. At first they carried flashlights but lately they've taken to wearing headlamps.

My neighbor Betti isn't happy about the situation. She stands on my porch, waving her extra-sharp tweezers in the air. She came over with a splinter lodged under her fingernail, and after a little poking around I got it out. It's the middle of the afternoon but she knew I'd be home. Now that the splinter is gone she's free to be irritated by other things, and my trash cans, lined up at the curb, have started her thinking about the recyclers. "I moved here to get away from this shit," she says, and even though she talks in kind of an ugly way, Betti is one of the most beautiful people I know.

She has arching eyebrows and the smallest possible pores, flat red lipstick that never rubs off on her teeth or crumbs up in the corners of her mouth. Shining dark hair smoothed back in a high ponytail. Toreador pants and little ballet flats so silvery and supple I hate to see them touching the sidewalk. The math still shocks me: she must be at least forty-five years old! You'd never know it, because her skin is amazing.

I used to look at her picture in magazines, ages ago, when I was a regular girl going to middle school and she was a popular person going to gay dance clubs in New York. Her friends were graffiti artists, punk bands, drag queens, rappers, gallery owners: everything was all mixed up then, in a good way. I used to read those magazines monkishly, over and over again, late into the night, as if they contained a key to unlocking a secret world of happiness. And maybe they did; maybe they taught me something important. Or maybe it was just a way to kill time until I could grow up, get a job, find a partner, buy a house—

A house four doors down from Betti Pérez! The houses are small but they cost a lot. What I mean is that they look sweet on the outside but there may be comedians or talent managers or people like Betti living inside.

"The other morning I'm standing in my kitchen," she

says, "still in my nightie, trying to get the toaster to work, and I hear something funny. A rustling-around kind of sound, like a rat makes? And I look over and there's a little man right outside my pantry window! Ten feet away from me! Digging away in there, helping himself."

"You should get your gate fixed," I tell her.

She raises her black eyebrows at me. "Don't make this my fault."

"Secure the perimeter, that's what Officer Cordova said."

"I'm trying to tell you a story."

"Didn't I give you Manuel's number?"

Betti scowls. "I'm going to get mad if you don't stop busting my balls."

A wave of happiness rushes over me. Here I am, fussing at Betti Pérez, and here she is, fussing back at me. I want to reach through time and squeeze the arm of my thirteen-year-old self: awake at one in the morning, sucking on Altoids, studying the captions in *PAPER* magazine . . .

Betti doesn't know that I liked her back when she was an underground queen of New York. She probably thinks I've seen her on the HBO show, or remember her from that recurring role on the one about the lawyers. The fact is, I don't watch too much TV, but there's no way I can say that around here without sounding ungracious.

"I wasn't wearing any panties," she says, suddenly thoughtful. "It made me feel sort of frozen in place. Like one of those bad dreams where you can't move your legs and you open your mouth but no words come out. The only thing I could do was grab my phone off the counter and shake it at him."

I tell her that the next time she should grab her phone and call Officer Cordova.

"The point is, they're not waiting for trash day anymore," Betti says. "The point is, they're *encroaching*."

On cue, my dog starts barking crazily from behind the picture window, as if he knows exactly what *encroaching* means. He's a big dog and his bark is loud, fast, and desperate. Though I've been living with him for over a year, his thinking remains mostly mysterious to me. I apologize to Betti and we look at my dog making a steady stream of sound, the wetness from his mouth spraying onto the glass. "Quiet, Hank," I say, but he ignores me, which isn't unusual for us. Betti says she has to leave. She's informed me before that when he barks, it's clearly audible at her house, even with her music on.

"Tell Amy I'm still waiting to hear from her," she says, leveling the tweezers at me, then she pivots on her soft silver shoes and walks away.

When I go back inside, my dog is lying attentively on the carpet, cheerful and calm, as if he truly has no idea who that maniac was, barking his head off.

I should say *our* dog, not *my* dog, because Amy and I adopted him together. We biked to the farmers' market one morning to buy some strawberries and salt and eggs and came home instead with a dog; they told us he was a shepherd mix but I suspect he's more mix than shepherd. The various rescue organizations are clever and set up shop all along the sidewalks on Sundays, so you can't buy a muffin or pick up your prescription without encountering at least a dozen beautiful animals needing homes. It's like running the gauntlet except instead of being pummeled with sticks you're pierced by the sad eyes of kittens and stray dogs, and the less expressive eyes of rabbits. There are always a couple of weeping children too, who want the animals but can't have them.

I wanted a child but couldn't have one, which is partly why we got the dog. Or maybe the dog is our warm-up to having a child—this is how Amy, who is plucky about nearly everything, looks at it. I'm the defeatist. I think the game's already over. I think of Hank as a consolation prize, a loud and needy consolation prize who sheds huge amounts of hair, but that could just be the hCG. Now that we've started on injectable cycles I've been feeling blue. "Get out," Amy tells me. "Take Hank for a hike." Which always seems like a reasonable idea until I try to execute it. Amy says that the problem is my car; if I had a bigger car it wouldn't be such a major production. She's been researching hybrid SUVs and threatening to take me on a test drive.

As for me, I don't want a bigger car. I miss the days when we didn't even own a car. I mean before we came to California, when we were still working crummy day jobs and living in New York. It used to take me twelve minutes to walk to the C/E station from our apartment on DeKalb. I used to bury my nose in my scarf and finger the smooth, flimsy MetroCard in my coat pocket and think about the magazine I would read once I got a seat on the train. Usually

I would read for only a few minutes before I fell asleep, lulled by the shaking train and the warmth of other people around me reading and sleeping. If I had to get to work early, I would walk the extra distance and take the D/Q line from Flatbush Avenue, just because I looked forward to the moment when the train emerged from the darkness to make its slow, rattling way across the bridge and the morning light would pour slantwise through the girders and spill over all of us sleeping inside the subway car, our hands folded and our heads nodding, me cracking my eyes open for only a second to see this and love this and then go back to dreaming.

The next time Betti appears on my porch she is holding a blue ice pack on top of her head. The rest of her is perfect: jersey wrap dress in navy, big gold hoops, long gold chains looped around her neck. She says that she needs me to see if she is bleeding.

"Should I take you to the hospital?" I ask, trying to keep Hank from wriggling past me and out the door. With all my blood tests I go to the hospital like a regular. "I know a great place to park."

"It's only a bump," Betti says. "I bumped my head like an idiot. You better get some hydrogen peroxide, just in case."

I find it in the downstairs bathroom along with a little plastic packet containing two quilted cotton pads that Amy must have taken from a fancy hotel. I think that Betti will like how neat and individually wrapped they are. She sits on the lower step of the porch and I sit on the higher one, leafing through her hair. She's released it from its ponytail.

"I don't even want to tell you how it happened. It's stupid, fucking stupid, and it's going to make me mad all over again."

But of course she tells me. She tells me that the little man came back. He startled her when she was wiping something off the kitchen floor and she stood up too quickly and banged her head on the corner of an open cabinet door.

"Really hard," she says. "I could practically see the stars and tweetie birds flying around. I did that concussion test, the one where you close your eyes and touch your nose. I'm okay in that regard."

I can't find a scratch anywhere. Just pale, clean scalp and the dark roots of her hair. I can see where she hit it, because the skin is pinker there and cold from the ice. But no blood. I split open the plastic packet and unscrew the cap from the bottle of peroxide. When I touch the wet pad to her head, Betti sighs with pleasure.

"Oh boy. I feel like I'm in the nurse's office at school. She used to go through our hair checking for lice. Every week, with her rubber gloves and a cotton ball soaked in alcohol." She laughs. "See? I told you I'm from the ghetto. That's what Catholic school was like in the Bronx. Back in the day!"

I love her so much. I don't even bother to ask if she has Manuel's number. I'm just going to call him myself, like I did when her sprinklers were flooding the sidewalk. Done: no more bottle-pickers breezing through her broken gate.

"Is it bad?" she asks soberly. "Is it deep?"

"It's nothing to worry about," I say, and smooth my hands over her shining hair.

"Thank you, bunny," she says, placing her ice pack back on her head, but now at an angle, like a beret. "It's hard living alone sometimes."

I know how she feels, even though technically I'm not living alone. Betti and her husband, Rick, split up six months ago. He's a contractor, with a show on a cable network where he rescues people from home improvement projects that have gone terribly wrong. It's called *DIY Undone*. It's funny because DIY used to mean something positive to me; it meant publishing your own magazine or starting a record label or making documentaries on borrowed cameras about homeless LGBT teenagers living in Morningside Park. Now DIY just makes me think of Rick and the look of relief on homeowners' faces when he pulls up in his vintage pickup truck. On the show he is heroically competent, but I've noticed that a lot of things at Betti's house don't work as well as they should, like the gate. He redid the whole house himself as a wedding present to her.

"You want to come inside?" I ask. "Everything's a mess."

Betti stands and studies Hank through the picture window, as if calculating how many dog hairs are going to attach themselves to her navy dress. "I've got a meeting. A big one, maybe. In Santa Monica."

I knock my knuckles against the nearest porch column. "I think this is wood."

"Speaking of which," Betti says, "has Amy said anything to you? I feel like I'm stalking her."

"Not yet." I wasn't expecting this, and now I have to pretend to sort through the contents of our mailbox. "She's super busy. Even more than normal. She hasn't even had time to do her laundry." Which doesn't sound very convincing, so I hear myself adding: "There's a huge pile of unwashed clothes stinking up the back of the closet."

I don't know why I offer this detail; why, in my panicked effort to make another person feel better, I always end up exposing Amy in an exaggerated and totally unnecessary way. The sickness I feel afterward somehow doesn't stop me from witlessly doing it again. Her adult ADD, her iffy eating habits, her dirty clothes . . .

Betti looks away, embarrassed—for Amy? for me? "She's seen my work, right?" Oh! For herself. It makes me want to hold her hand. "You think I should tell my agent to send over some DVDs?"

"No! Don't. We're really big fans." My voice gets a little throaty from the relief of finally saying it. And it doesn't seem wrong in the moment to say *we*, even though I'm actually just speaking for myself. "We love you. We've loved you forever."

"Seriously?" Betti asks. She smiles, her face opening. Everything about her softens a little. "You guys. You kill me."

"Like, forever."

We grin at each other. I want to tell her that she's the reason I moved to New York.

"So you get why this is such a good idea," she says, before I have my chance. She removes the ice pack from her head and leans in as if she's telling me something new. "It's a no-brainer. It's my retirement fund."

For a while she's been wanting to pitch a kids' show to Amy, because that's what Amy makes: half-hour television shows for kids. And that's how we get to live in this house! To be clear, Amy's show is not the educational kind, it's more like the kind that parents complain about, but the writing is smart and these kids are lovely to watch, bright-eyed and funny and quick. Real actors, grown up now, with serious careers, have gotten their start on this kind of show. What I'm trying to say is that it's not dreck, and Amy turns out to be very talented at it, even though it's given her sciatica and a sleeping disorder. How does a slightly graying lesbian documentary maker know exactly what eight-to-twelve-year-old girls will enjoy watching while curled up in their beanbags, eating snacks? "It's my uncanny ability," Amy likes to say, half joking and half amazed. But we're just like those girls; we've always been interested in teenagers too, so maybe it's not such a leap after all.

In Betti's show there'll be two teenagers—the finicky older brother and the gorgeous, unmanageable sister—and then a couple of younger siblings thrown in for laughs and relatability. Betti's plan is that one of the little ones will be an adopted kid from Asia or Africa. Or even better, both of them could be adopted! But definitely from different continents. Anyway, four kids at the very least, though she's open to more. And an uptight, standoffish dad—think

Captain von Trapp as a captain of industry—plus probably one more adult for good measure: A Scottish housekeeper with fluffy hair? A snooty building manager? Someone to balance out Betti—because the whole idea is that Betti's character isn't really an adult. She's the wildly inappropriate babysitter.

Former denizen of downtown clubs, former B-girl, former hairdresser, former bad girl from the Bronx, with the accent to boot: guess who's taking care of the kids! She's faked her résumé; she has no business doing this; all she's got is a tube of Chanel lipstick and her street smarts. When they push her, she'll push back. Sass, life lessons, more sass. Thrift-store shopping, gum snapping, wisecracking, popping and locking. In the pilot she'll enter the little ones in a citywide dance contest.

It makes sense, I can see that. I can see the appeal. Objectively it's not sillier or more overcooked than any other show on Amy's network. But the idea of Betti pausing for a laugh track still makes me more depressed than I can say.

She reminds me that the concept has already been done, which is apparently what makes it such a sure bet now. "That went for six full seasons," she says, "and ended a decade ago. It's way overdue for a relaunch." She hoots to hear herself talking this way. "Jesus Christ! I sound like my fucking manager."

"He isn't concerned," I ask, "about going in a different direction? Because the stuff Amy does, it's not exactly—"

"My manager! Please. He'll pimp me out for any old thing." Betti gives me her ice pack so she can use both of her hands as she's talking. "And so what if it's not high art? I did that. I made those movies. I love independent film as much as the next girl. The first film I ever did? It went to Cannes and came *this* close to winning a Palme d'Or. So what have I got to prove? I like working. I like making money. I've got a mother I want to take care of. Is Rick still paying the mortgage on that house? I don't think so. And most people don't know this, but HBO residuals are shit. So what this show's not going to Cannes. You want to criticize me for trying to get my hustle on? Fuck you. Someone's got to pay my bills."

I think I must look a little stunned, because Betti touches my arm.

"Oh bunny, I didn't mean *you*. It's just a colorful expression."

"I know that," I tell her. "I say it sometimes for emphasis too."

"You're funny." Betti shakes her head and walks down the steps, sending a goodbye wave over her shoulder. "Now all we have to do is come up with a name." She looks back at me like she's not sure I've been keeping up with her. "For the show!"

It's two days later when Manuel rings the doorbell. His white truck is in the driveway, its bed stacked with cedar planks. After saying hello, I point down the street. "It's Betti's gate," I remind him, "not ours."

"Surprise!" He laughs softly. "I'm here for *you*." I notice how young he looks with his new haircut, and I notice the pleasant, artificial scent of laundry soap that his shirts always let off at the beginning of the day. If we lived in New York, and I had taken a seat next to him on the subway, I might have fallen asleep on his shoulder.

He keeps patting his front pocket, even though his cell phone isn't in there. He tells me that he's going to build a chicken coop in my backyard.

I can't help repeating it. "A chicken coop? In our yard?"

But he's already back by his truck, hoisting planks onto his shoulder.

"Is this Amy's idea?" I call out.

He nods, which is difficult to do with all the wood that he's balancing. "She wants to give you a surprise."

"I didn't think Amy even had your number," I say pointlessly. I'm still trying to get my bearings. "You talked about where she wants to put it?" I ask as I follow him down the driveway.

Without grunting, he deposits the first load onto the grass. "I think you'll like it," he says. When he straightens, he pauses for a moment, then smiles. "The dog is quiet today."

It's true. Hank is miraculously silent. Usually he goes bonkers whenever Manuel or any other male sets foot on the porch, or the driveway, or especially when someone dares to venture into the backyard. "He's getting to know you," I say brightly, but I am disturbed. His insane barking is what reminds me that Hank has a past, and memories from a time before we knew him. I can't understand why he is now soundlessly watching us through the glass of the back door.

Manuel says that the coop will be big enough to hold six chickens. "That's many eggs," he observes, and I inwardly sicken, and it occurs to me then that neither he nor Amy has any idea what a bad, bad joke this whole urban-agrarian cedarwood surprise is. I gaze at him dumbly as he digs his little dowels into the ground and then uses string to mark off the dimensions of the chicken structure. I know Manuel is just doing what Amy asked him to do, and I know Amy is just trying to keep me balanced and upbeat, but think about it: while she's out in Burbank making kids' shows, and the chickens are out in the backyard making eggs, I'll be in the kitchen making rosemary cookies to bring as a gift to my reproductive endocrinologist. Sometimes, as I'm sanding the cookies with granulated sugar or sticking myself in the stomach with a disposable needle, it's hard to remember that I used to make other things, and who cares if in the end they never found distribution, I made them. Amy and I made them together.

"Knock knock," says a voice coming down the driveway, a voice so recognizable that Betti has wondered aloud on occasion why she doesn't yet have a voice-over career. "What are you kids doing back here? I saw the truck."

Betti's shoes are very pointy in the toes and high in the heels, so she can't step onto the grass to take a closer look at the construction site. "Where the heck do you get the chickens from?" she asks.

"I have no idea." I sink into a stackable chair left over from our last cookout. "Though I imagine Amy already has somebody working on it."

I say it so dryly that I surprise myself.

"You be nice!" Betti says, aiming a tapered red fingernail at me. "I finally got a meeting with her. Next Monday, and I'm a fucking nervous wreck, and I couldn't have done it without you."

She dips her hand wrist-deep into her purse and delicately shifts things around until her hand reappears, flourishing a business card. "I'm giving you a session with my acupuncturist. He's going to seriously help you. He says no more cold drinks. No ice cream." She passes me the card and heads for my back door. "You got to keep everything nice and warm in there. Okay? Like a greenhouse. Don't move; I'm getting you a cup of hot water."

To her credit, Betti opens the door only a crack and inches herself through sideways, but Hank is fast and unfathomable, and after all that weird stillness and silence at the back door he now squirms past her and comes hurtling out into the yard. Manuel and I freeze. The last time this happened it was bad. Manuel said afterward that it was okay, it was just the edge of his shirt, an old shirt, but I'm not so sure I believe him. I was straddling Hank and gripping his choke collar and both the dog and I were panting. I don't think Manuel told me everything in that moment, and I failed to ask him about it again. But today Hank goes right past him, past the cedar planks, past the paloverde tree and the big bank of native grasses, straight down to the fence, where he begins to sniff about with a frantic sort of urgency.

"I was nervous there for a second," I say, half laughing, ashamed. "My fault!" Betti calls from behind us. "Everyone all right?" Without comment, Manuel stands formally and adjusts his position so that he can keep his eye on the dog as he works.

I watch Hank patrol the fence, his nose to the ground, snuffling in and around the wood chips. When we first had the plantings installed, we thought Hank was chewing on the leaves and making himself sick. While walking across our new yard, Amy and I would find large puddles of vomit sitting neatly on top of the mulch. We decided we had to keep Hank shut inside, we had to live with his miserable yelping and barking and door-scratching, me more than Amy because I'm the one who's at home with him, and still we continued to wake up and find the foamy yellow pools scattered among the plantings. This led to escalating passive-aggressive insinuations about who was breaking the rules, and when that got us nowhere, to the reconciliatory writing of an angry letter to the neighbor (not Betti, who's allergic) about her failure to contain her nauseous cat. Thank God Manuel stopped us before we slipped the letter under her door. "It's alive," he told us, and sure enough, there it was on the internet, even yellower than ours, with a name that was gross, funny, sublimely exact: dog vomit slime mold. Truly! It pops up overnight, like magic, spreading spore and discord. But now with the drought we don't see it anymore.

Betti returns, carrying two steaming cups, and drags over another chair. "Salud," she says. She taps her mug to mine. "Don't get excited. I'm way too old. I'm just keeping you company."

It feels strange to be drinking something hot that doesn't have any flavor. I wonder if I should offer some to Manuel. I always offer him sodas or lemonade or filtered ice water, and he almost always refuses. He says he keeps a cooler in his truck.

Betti's talking earnestly again about her show. "*The Caregiver*. Too heavy, right? And I kind of liked *The Giver*, but then my manager told me that's the name of a book the kids all have to read in school."

"*The Sitter*?" I ask.

"I like that, I thought of that too. My manager says it sounds like a horror movie franchise. Then I had a dream and the name *Sitter City* came to me in the dream and I figured that was a sign, that was it, but after a day of loving this name I ultimately realized that it sounds like there are *lots* of sitters on the show, an entire city of sitters, when in fact it's only me. *I'm* the sitter."

"*Sitter in the City*—"

"And that was my major breakthrough: me! Why not embrace it? There's a great tradition."

She takes a long, careful sip of her water and looks at me expectantly over the rim of her cup.

I hesitate. "You want to call the show *Betti*?"

She stomps her right foot, and her pointy heel sinks into the space between the pavers. "How did you know!"

For a moment it's unclear whether she's angry or delighted.

"It works, right?" She bends down and extracts her shoe. "It was staring us in the face the whole time. I mean, think about it: *Alice, Maude, Rhoda, Phyllis . . .*"

"*Betti*," I say. "It's easy to remember."

"Right? Pretty catchy. I'm so fucking relieved. I mean, it's the name of my character, Betti Escobedo," she clarifies modestly, "and even though it's an ensemble cast, she's the heart of the show."

"*Betti*," I repeat, and she lets out a sigh.

I look over: She isn't kidding. She is genuinely relieved. She is in fact awash in relief: eyes closed, head dropped back in her chair, face turned to the sun. All it took was a name? A meeting with Amy, and a name? This is the closest I've ever come to seeing Betti in a state of rest. You could even say she looks at peace, though not in a dead way.

But the relief does do something strange to Betti's face. For the first time I see a trace of looseness there. Tipped back, at rest, it reminds me of what a circus tent might look like from a distance in the split second after the tent poles have been pulled down by the carnies. The tent hasn't started to sink yet, but you can see that it's just about to. That last moment of tension before everything gently ripples, then gives way. Now this is a ridiculous comparison for me to make because I've never in my life seen such a thing occur, and I don't even know if they dismantle the tent poles first, or if carnies are the ones to do it, or if that's even the correct word for people who work behind the scenes at a circus. But it seems easier to imagine a sight I've never seen before than it is to notice the slight heaviness under her jaw, or how her foundation lies dustily on top of her skin. Pouching. Crepey. Horrible words! Criminal to even think them in a sentence.

I sip my hot water and try to visualize my warm, humid interiors. I can't tell if this is an inane or a marvelous thing to be doing. I guess, like Betti's face, that its integrity depends on the angle you see it from. Because in some lights my life appears grotesque to me. Here I am sitting in the sun, holding a mug and having a chat as if there isn't a man on his hands and knees just a few yards away from me, being paid to do something I could very well do myself, something I could be doing instead of half listening to the career plans of an aging character actress as we both gaze absently at the manic, aimless behavior of my traumatized rescue dog. What a ludicrous scene! So absurd and rotten. So disgusting that it makes me want to throw up—yes—right there on the mulch.

But the thought of dog vomit slime mold cheers me up a bit. As Manuel said, it's alive. It's part of a much bigger system, all of it growing and decomposing and feeding off one another. And sometimes, if I tilt my thinking a little to one side, I feel like I live a magical life and am part of a huge and beautiful system. I think about the chickens I'm going to raise, and the healthy child I'm going to have one day. I think about the people at night with their head-lamps and how I'm supporting a struggling economy just by putting out my recycling every week. I think what a blessing it is to be drinking hot water with Betti Pérez, who seems as wonderful to me now as she did twenty-five years ago, when she was operating the hand-crank elevator at Danceteria.

One of Amy's favorite phrases to say to me is "Don't overthink it." She says it when I get flustered and worked up over something. She said it when we were deciding to buy this house, and when we redid the landscaping, and again when we were standing on the sidewalk, looking at Hank huddled inside a plastic crate. And in most cases, she's been right. The dog, for instance. He's crazy and un-knowable, but he loves us absolutely. When he's not acting in an alarming way, he's a great comfort to be around. It can make me happy simply to watch him, like now. He lopes easily back and forth across the yard—once, twice, three times, ignoring Manuel all the while, then finding a spot that he likes near the fence, he settles back on his haunches, collapses onto his side, stretches out his front legs, and lays his head down on the grass. My good boy.

"Guess what." Betti's eyes open; her head pops up. "My little man came back! And this time he actually smiled at me."

All her old indignation has turned into high spirits. Again, Amy? What an effect. But now I am the one who feels relieved: Betti's face has come back into focus.

"And you know what? He has a humongous gap between his front teeth. You could drive a truck through there."

"I thought Manuel—"

At the sound of his name, Manuel glances over at us, alert.

"Oh, he did. He did. The gate's working again. It's fine." Betti waves at him. "Thank you, Manuel!" She says his name not like I do but with a good accent, the *a* sounding as if it's been flattened by the warm palm of someone's hand.

Then, without warning, they begin speaking to each other in Spanish. Energetically, as if they have a lot to express. I didn't know before now that Betti could speak Spanish, and at some points I'm uncertain if she actually can or if she's just delivering a few key words with the help of many eloquent hand gestures. I wonder if they're discussing the gate repair, because in the midst of their back-and-forth I hear my own name, but soon I think that the scope of their conversation is wider than that, because occasionally I catch Amy's name too. Listening to them talk about us but not understanding what they're saying doesn't feel as bad as you might think; in fact it feels like pulling a blanket up to your chin and resting underneath it.

Betti says something that makes the two of them laugh. "He's being nice to me. I can barely put a sentence together." She gives Manuel another wave. "But we agree. The gate doesn't really make a difference, bunny."

Her chair scrapes against the pavers as she scoots closer.

"According to him, a gate doesn't do shit!" she says gaily. "I get it. The little man's just trying to handle his business. Just doing what he's got to do." She leans across and pokes me in the arm. "I bet he likes eggs."

She winks at me. Now she looks perfectly herself again: immaculate, ironclad, ready for anything.

THE YOUNG WIFE'S TALE

There once was a king who came to his throne only after a long period of trouble. Everyone, everywhere, felt relief that he had at last returned to them, but no one felt it more keenly than the young wives of the men whom he led. What possessed them was more than relief; it was a deep, mysterious joy. Their husbands would no longer be leaving for war, they told themselves. Their children would grow old under the eyes of their fathers, and the land would prosper, and life would be restored to the rhythms they could not even recall. So they said to one another as they bent their heads and pounded clothes in the cold streams.

In truth, the young wives were stirred by the king's bravery, and his extraordinary beauty. Never before had they seen a man as beautiful as he. They wondered whether it was the years in exile, his time spent wandering disguised and alone, that had given him his grace. His eyes said he understood all the sadness in the world, and his worn face said that he would do everything in his power to defeat it. These qualities, combined with his dark, lank hair and his roughened hands, made the young wives almost frantic with a longing they couldn't describe. But they would see it reflected in each other's flushed, stricken faces, and know that they were not alone in what they felt.

The women's hunger caused them to act in strange ways. Some small, some not. One wife awoke in the morning, climbed from the bed, went about her tasks, and heated the water, without once opening her eyes. She was reluctant to enter out of her dream. Another, in the early days of winter, would slip behind her house, take off her clothes, and stand turned to the sun, unmoving as stone. Among the youngest of the wives was a girl who disappeared for long spells into the forest. Each time she would eat a little less and roam a little farther, in the belief that she might faint at just the moment the king was striding past, and he would stoop down to the ground, lift her up in his arms, and revive her. Why she believed this was a mystery—the king did not hunt in these woods, nor did he travel alone anymore, nor did he travel on foot. Maybe she was searching for the exiled king, the sorrowful king, and believed she would find him in this forest. But he would be at once the king adrift and the king redeemed, because look, in her dream, how he lifts her from the ground.

In time, the king died and passed into legend. He was remembered in songs and paintings and books, and then for a long while he was forgotten, as the paintings blackened and the books moldered and other, shorter songs came into fashion. Such a very long time went by, it seemed possible that the king and his hard struggles, the peace that followed, would be forever lost, as if his beauty had never existed, and he had never walked this earth or looked up at this sky. But there was an old university where, one night, a scholar discovered the king, either in a trance or in the stacks of the library, and once again his story came to light. First, he appeared in sketches and drafts, then in a book so long it required multiple volumes, followed by rock-and-roll albums and animated cartoons, underground fanzines and doctoral dissertations, and, finally, a film.

In this latest incarnation, the king began again to disturb the young wives of the world. There were so many pleasures to be had as a young wife—the new towels and sheets, the espresso machine, the warm, receptive body waiting in the bed—and at first this seemed merely one of them. Two women together, confessing the terrible love they felt for their husbands, so much deeper and sharper than they had ever expected to feel, could then pour fresh cups of coffee, pick up crumbs off the new yellow dishes with the moistened tips of their fingers, and proceed to speak gravely of their feelings for the king without suffering the slightest twinge of foolishness or betrayal. They took it as one of the privileges of marriage. They laughed when other women, their still-unmarried friends, suggested it was a movie actor who provoked in them their peculiar hunger. Because hadn't they seen him a hundred times before, as a cowboy drifter, an army sergeant, a sidekick, a painter having an affair? It was not an actor who stirred them. Their thoughts belonged wholly to the brave, ravaged, beautiful king.

———————

Eva believed in the beginning that the king reminded her of her husband, and she told him so. He smiled at her in such a way to show he was grateful, but also that he disagreed. Don't you see it? Eva asked. She was full of adoration for him. For the way his feet sounded coming up the stairs, the way he kept himself so clean-smelling and neat, for the solo dances he'd perform on the carpet when he was happy. Countless ways and things she adored, innumerable as the stars. Things that of course existed before they were married, but to which she could now fully surrender, abandoning herself to wonder. How did she ever. How did she ever. She could not account for her fortune. She could only note that she had, unaware, held part of her self in suspension before, and now she had let go. The fall was slow, luxurious, and seemingly infinite. It refused to be described. She was reduced to murmuring, almost against her will, You are the best. Words impoverished of their meaning, used most often to thank a person to whom one's not truly indebted, but when Eva uttered them to her husband, she asked the words to carry the full weight of her astonishment. She wasn't ever confident they did.

A paradox of growing so close to another person was the doubt that you could impart to them the very closeness that you felt. Eva would awake in the night, feeling someone's breath on her forehead, hearing someone beside her ask, Do you know how much your husband loves you? Do you know?

Eva would sigh and burrow more deeply next to him, then descend into a dream about the king. He was drawing his sword from his belt. He was turning to face an enemy. The look on his face was grim, and the circle of motion his body described—rough hand on hilt, arm sweeping up, torso pivoting in the direction of danger—had a poem's grace, its balance and frugality. There was the clang of metal meeting. The hissing sound of tempered weapons slicing through the air. More enemies, their black helmets dull in the brilliant sunlight, came swarming down the wooded slope. They yelped and they whooped, they beat their drums and bared their rotting teeth like dogs, but the expression on the king's face did not change. One by one he felled his enemies, pressing in on him from all sides, with a bleak patience and determination. Eva flattened herself against a tree and quaked. Not once in her dream did she fear for the king, but she felt acutely the overwhelming odds against him, the extreme peril, the thrill. He would not die, but he might come close. The bark of the tree bit into her skin, her fingers were sticky with pitch, the pine needles yielded beneath her feet. The next time that Eva awoke, in the darkness of the bedroom, her heart was beating very fast.

The mornings made her sad. She didn't like saying goodbye to her husband when he left for work. She held on to him tightly, and he said to her, We'll see each other tonight. I know, she sighed, but that seems far away from now. And it was true, the days were long. He was a resident in emergency medicine. He was a lawyer for legal aid. He wrote articles about changes in technology, for which he was paid, and also articles about wars in Africa, for which he was not paid. He worked in a record shop and composed strange, haunting music. It didn't matter. He was doing something good. Eva, also, had a job. She had high hopes for herself. For both of them. They were traveling the distance, in very small, sometimes imperceptible increments, between where they found themselves now and where they desired one day to be. Soon. It wasn't happening quickly enough. You're getting there, they told each other. With brightness in their voices, a true conviction. Over and over they told each other, You're a rock star. Fuck them. What do they know. You're kicking ass. I mean it. We're getting there. Soon.

Eva would see the king when she stepped onto the bus in the mornings. Then she would see him again in the lap of the little boy sitting across from her on the aisle. She would see him behind the glass at the newsstand, and as he flew raggedly down the length of a block. When she walked to the bank she saw him, hair tangled and sword raised, looking out across the city from the top of an office building. Somehow he remained irreducibly himself, even when miniaturized on a lunch box, or multiplied in the pages of a magazine, or flattened and stretched across the side of a bus. Though she saw him everywhere, her spirit would still leap in surprise at the sight of him. Then her heart would unfurl, in petals of flame, and she would burn with a clear, consuming light.

At its peak, before it extinguished itself, the fire made Eva's vision sharpen. She perceived what was beautiful and fierce in the man who drove the bus, his supple fingers tapping against the wheel, and the man beside her in the elevator, who nodded at her kindly, almost caressingly, before he stepped off at the seventh floor, and the man she saw from her window, crossing the street against the traffic light, a small limp in his step. She stared at each of them and realized, I could love you. The thought filled her with courage. She wondered if everyone around her might feel it, her valor and love, radiating off her like heat. But as quickly as it flared up, her insight faded, and all that remained were the ashes, the unremarkable faces of men.

The nights also made Eva sad sometimes. She tried luring her husband into staying up late, with the promise of movies or cookie dough or card games. I don't want to go to sleep yet, she'd say as her eyelids grew heavier and heavier. Yet the new sheets were so exquisitely soft. And the blanket her cousins had brought back from Wales. Their bed was an abyss into which she could not help but precipitously fall. She clasped his arm, knowing that to sleep was to leave each other for a while. I'll be right here, he said. I'm not going anywhere. And she said wistfully, I know! Sleep well. I'll see you in the morning.

Her husband shook his head. She could hear his hair rubbing back and forth on the pillowcase. I'll probably see you before then, he said. You have a funny habit of showing up in my dreams. You're always hanging around.

He said it with exasperation, but he didn't mean it. Together they had developed a talent for hanging around. How else could they have built their wealth of solace and closeness and ease? They lived surrounded by the dear familiar. Eva had been folding laundry when he asked her to marry him. He had been warming leftover noodles on the stove. On the television played a spooky show that they liked, whose characters and conflicts they knew so well, had seen so many times, that they could drift in and out of conversation, or become absorbed with the task of mating socks, of stirring pans, to still return and feel they hadn't missed anything at all. When Eva turned around to glance at the screen, she nearly fell over her husband (not yet her husband), who was on his knees among the washcloths and the turtlenecks still spread across the floor. He opened his hand, like a magician about to make a coin disappear, and there sat a ring. Her grandmother's ring; she recognized it at once. But how did it ever end up in his hand? There had been forethought, conspiracy! Her very soul rushed forward to meet him. She dropped to the floor and they held each other, laughing and weeping, with all the beloved things of their life arrayed about them, the butter popping in the pan, the detective muttering on the television, the water stain from the leak last winter floating on the ceiling above their heads.

Recounting the moment later, she shivered at the possibility that it could have happened differently. I would have been embarrassed! she cried. A dimly lit restaurant, a horse-drawn carriage? A banner pulled by a propeller plane across the sky? Some women she knew had become engaged on faraway beaches, strolling underneath the moon. Ugh, she said. It was horrible to contemplate. There were so many opportunities for the process to go awry. She felt lucky her husband had asked the right way, the solely acceptable way, which was exactly the way that he had.

But saying so was obvious. For if he had asked in a different manner, if he had taken her to the top of a mountain, or buried the ring in a chocolate dessert, then he would have been a different person, and she would never have married him, now would she.

Would she?

With a pang she remembered the dizzying sensation she had felt while walking through the city. Anything was possible. Anything, more dangerously, was imaginable. Why was it so easy to feel the bus driver's hand holding her own as he led her up the crumbling stoop to meet his father? And how did she know that the man on the elevator preferred his eggs soft in the middle, served on little dry triangles of toast? Every glance, every encounter, contained within it a dark, expanding universe of intimacies, exploding like dandelion fluff at her slightest breath, flying up and drifting about and taking stubborn root somewhere. Which was why she understood, with absolute certainty, that the slightly lame, foolhardy fellow, the one riskily crossing the street, would, if given the chance, bury his head between her legs, inhale, and utter indecipherable words of joy, making every inch of her vibrate with the sound.

Did you hear me?

Yes, yes, I heard you, she says, and sinks her hands into the damp head of hair, lightly closing her eyes, feeling her body hum, wondering how did she ever—

Eva?

Her husband was propped up on his elbow, looking at her curiously.

You asleep? he asked.

That night she dreamed once more of the king. He heaved open the oaken doors to the hall and hung there, his bent figure thrown into shadow, before he staggered through. The men gathered in the great hall stopped what they were doing and turned to him and stared. They seemed hardly to recognize their king, his face filthy, his eyes haggard, his lean body stooped with exhaustion and pain. It was as if they could scarcely believe he was not dead. A young boy was the first to come to his senses and run forward to the king, who hesitated, then laid his hand, with a sigh, upon the child's shoulder. Rousing themselves from their disbelief, the men sent up a shout. The king had come home. His enemies, who had snatched him from the battlefield, could not keep him. The voices of his men echoed through the hall, but the king did not share in their rejoicing. He smiled at them faintly. Leaning on the boy, he limped to a dark corner, sank down on a bench, tipped his head back against the stone, and closed his eyes. Eva stood pressed behind a pillar, close enough to see how his face twitched with grief. She looked down and found she was carrying a basin of water, its cool weight trembling slightly in her hands. The water, she knew, was meant for the king. But before she could move to him, a hush fell over the hall, the men parting as another walked slowly through their midst and with quiet steps approached the body resting on the bench. The man was tall, his hair gray, and when he stood before the king, he seemed to cover him with light. My lord, the man said, in a voice of such gentleness that the king then opened his eyes. His face showed his struggle to understand what he saw. You fell, the king whispered. The older man looked at him with love. Yes, the man said, but I did not die. And from the king's face the pain dropped away, and wonder took its place, for his old friend had been returned to him.

The moment was broken by the sound of water dripping. Eva gazed down at the bowl in her hands. Then she awoke, in the darkness of the bedroom, feeling wetness on her cheeks, pooled in the cups of her ears. She heard a voice beside her whispering. Eva, it said. Eva, it asked in soft dismay, why are you crying?

In the morning, it was her husband who held on tightly. He looked back up at her as he circled down the stairs. When he reached the bottom, out of sight, he called to her, as if he wasn't sure she'd still be there. He told her to have a very good day. He told her to say hello for him to her friend. I will, she shouted into the stairwell, I will. The front door scraped open, lingered a moment, and then swung shut with a gasp.

As her husband had asked, Eva delivered his special hello to her friend. She was a young wife herself, and pregnant. Her doctor had offices in the part of the city where

Eva worked, so after her appointment they would sometimes meet at a restaurant and eat together. Generally speaking, her friend had an exceptional appetite, but now she stared down sadly at her food.

She said, I bet this looks delicious to you.

Eva shook her head.

What? Her friend lit up. Are you pregnant too?

Eva shook her head again, and smiled.

Oh. Her friend subsided. You got my hopes up. I thought for a minute I wasn't alone.

You're not alone, Eva said.

She found her friend disturbing to behold. Her face appeared both drawn and puffy at the same time. Tiny blossoms of burst blood vessels had broken out along her cheeks and the delicate skin above her breasts. Her hair— all over, she said—had turned coarser. All day she stroked her stomach without knowing it, though her belly had only just emerged.

We have a favorite, she said. I want to know what you think. Lucy.

I like it, Eva said. And what if it's a boy?

Her friend spoke the musical name of the king, and a shudder passed between them.

Can you imagine? her friend asked, for a moment on fire. She remembered herself. No, really it's Jack.

I like that too, Eva said.

The waiter took their plates away, untouched.

Her friend dropped her head into her hands. I'm tired, she said. How did this happen to me? I'm tired all the time.

Eva didn't know what to say. She reached across the table and rested her hand on the woman's arm.

Her friend glanced up, brightened, and then began to scold. You didn't eat anything. That's unforgivable. You're going to disappear before our eyes. Don't you dare do that when I'm blowing up like a balloon.

After they had finished wrapping themselves in their coats and their scarves, her friend kissed her on both cheeks. One is for you, she said, and the other is for him.

As her friend had asked, Eva bestowed a kiss upon her husband. He was already asleep when she came home. She lit a candle and studied him as he lay sleeping in their bed. He too possessed his own share of beauty, or so she had thought in the beginning, and so she was repeatedly still told. Many people, men and women both, found his looks worth noting. But she could no longer see it. She saw only the face most familiar to her, most dear. Over time, her tender stare had drifted over his face and settled there—on his forehead, his eyelids, his cheekbones, his mouth—hiding from her what was beautiful in him.

She had thought, like Psyche, like all the other curious young wives, that she might creep up on her husband while he lay unconscious, a small circle of light hovering in her hand, and spy the secret face that had for so long remained invisible to her. Psyche had believed she would find a serpent. Another wife, a troll. And what did they find but Beauty. Their fair husbands had vanished like smoke. But why should Eva think of those old stories? The magnificent castles, the unseen servants. Imagine those wives in an apartment!

Could enchantment take hold among the milk crates, the sickly houseplants, the student-loan statements? When the match sparked and the wick flared, all Eva saw was her husband's face, neither stunning nor monstrous. The face that she loved. Wax did not drip from her candle; the spell went unbroken. He stayed right where he was, fast asleep.

For the first time, the king appeared alone in Eva's dream, standing atop a dry and windy hill. His cloak flapped roughly about his legs, and above him the sky glowed with a strange luminosity. Heavy gray clouds moved low and swift over a scrim of sheer, pearly, roseate light. The clouds were edged in gold and vermilion, and seemed to portend that some stirring, unknowable change was on its way. But the king did not gaze at the mysterious sky, the dark gilded clouds sweeping overhead. He kept his eyes fixed on the barren ground. He ran his open hand over a brittle tuft of grass, he turned a small stone over with his boot. Suddenly he fell to his knees, his cloak gusting up behind him, and brought his face close to the turf. What he found excited him. Hurrying on in an urgent, uneven gait, half scrambling, half running, trying to stay low to the ground, the king followed a path of signs discernible only to him. Eva could not guess what he was seeking. Her perspective was puzzling: in one blink she saw the king as a distant figure, stark against the roiling sky, and in another she could see the tiny flecks of brightness in the stone he overturned. Where am I? she wondered, and at the very moment the question arose, she felt beneath her palms the cool, papery surface of a birch. She was lost in a stand of ravishingly white, naked trees. And at the very moment she knew she was lost, she also understood she would be found. It was she the king was searching for. Stepping through the pale trees, their white arms touching her, she drew closer and closer until at last she appeared on the edge of the wood, the wind filling her nightgown like a sail. The king looked up from the ground and saw her.

Then Eva awoke, in the darkness of the bedroom. Her heart had slowed to a languorous throb. She felt as if she was surfacing from a sleep that resembled, or perhaps preceded, death. She wanted to reach for the hand of her husband, but found herself too entranced, too abandoned, to do so. Though she could not lift her head, she became dimly aware of a reddish gleam at the foot of the bed, and wondered if, having dreamed this dream, she was destined to go up in flames, the bed a pyre, a shimmering blanket of fire enfolding her. But she was not. Through the low-ered veil of her lashes, she made out embers burning in a grate; through the remnants of her dream, she smelled the ancient scent of woodsmoke, she heard the ticking of cinders falling into ash. Opening her eyes, she saw above her a low ceiling, black beams of wood, a small window hanging bright and faceted as a jewel. The room was not her own. Her husband was not beside her.

In the first days of the king's return, there was a girl who wandered far into the forest. At dusk she would come home, with scratched face and torn skirts and brambles stuck like pins in her hair, to find her husband sitting before a hearth gone cold, a pot caked with old gruel. But how his eyes would shine when she appeared! He draws out her seat, he brings in water, he makes her a broth, which she plays with, with her spoon. She smiles at him shyly, saying, I think I lost my sense of time.

One evening, the dusk turns into darkness and still the girl has not come home. Her husband runs to the edge of the forest, a torch in his hand. All night he searches for her, the legions of trees looming around him, and by morning he stumbles out from the woods, bewildered and afraid, having found no sign of her. The other wives are washing clothes in the stream. They bend down farther over their work, as if by doing so they might make themselves invisible. The young husband approaches them, his face a wound, his voice hoarse when he asks them, Have you seen her? The women, up to their elbows in cold water, shake their heads. They are silent.

Eva imagined the silence into which her husband would awake. She imagined his voice in the empty room, saying her name. She heard, clearly, the variations he would use—Evita? Evuncular?—time's elaborations, the joyful, thoughtless ornamenting of the word he most liked to say. The names would chime and shiver in the air. Evel Knievel? he would ask, and there would be no answer. She had been taken too far away.

In a strange bed, in a strange room, she felt the anguish of her husband as her own. It felt like knives, like rats gnawing, like broken glass, like poison bubbling—no, it felt like something else. Exactly. All it took was two slippery pills, swallowed at the clinic, and then a bus ride home and straight into bed. The pain began as a little pang in her gut, and then—whoosh!—she was possessed by it. Her husband (not yet her husband) knelt beside the bed with a cool washcloth in his hand as she writhed around like a snake, sweating through the sheets. And just as swiftly it was over. The pain disappeared and the bleeding began. The whole thing lasted only an afternoon. In the evening the two of them walked around the neighborhood, eating ice cream. To say they had made a decision would suggest that they had needed to have a conversation. Neither one had said, Given the smallness of our apartment, and the narrowness of the stairs. Considering where we are in our lives . . . She didn't even have to mention her wedding dress, which was already paid for, already fitted, sitting hugely and steadfastly on her credit card. It was made of silk organza and floated up behind her when she moved. It was the color of champagne.

In this strange bed, in this close room, beneath the tiny jewel of a window, she thought of her husband and felt again the ache of that dreamlike afternoon. Or at least she did for a little while. A shockingly, shamefully little while. For how could she stay sad when the king himself was watching her, sitting alert by the fire? As she saw his dark eyes gleaming in the light, her sorrow for her husband dwindled into a low, melancholy note above which her false heart trilled. The king! The brave and ravaged and beautiful king. What might he say to her? What might he see? There was always the possibility he could love her, wasn't there? There was always the possibility. If her young marriage had taught her anything, it was that. The surprise, the stark miracle of love, bent in her direction. So why not the king, watching silently from his chair?

She felt his eyes move over her, touching each part of her deliberately, like a hand.

The next time Eva awoke, in the darkness of the bedroom, her heart was brimming, beating lightly as a bird's. The heaviness that had pulled on her was lifted. She yawned enormously, stretching her limbs to the far corners of the bed. At the end of the room a ruddy light glowed, but rising up onto her elbows, she saw that it belonged to the unsteady streetlamp outside her apartment window. And above her was her ceiling, still haunted by the water stain. The crooked blinds. The seething radiator. Did the sound of its spitting mean she was back? The dream over? More likely, more tormenting, the dream continued, and she had simply been ejected from it. For there sat her umbrella, her shoes. There lay the novel she was reading, prostrate on the floor. Her crumpled socks. His swaybacked boots. His corduroy pants, upright and perfectly accordioned. They spoke of the lovely, unflustered motion with which he had loosened them, allowed them to drop down the length of his legs, neatly stepped clear of them, and then plunged into the bed. Her husband. His watch resting on the bureau. His stack of *National Geographic*s. The photograph of his mother and father and sisters on the wall. His harmonica glinting. His collection of fortune-cookie fortunes in a jar. All the things about him she adored, infinite and ordinary as the stars.

She reached for his hand. She slid her foot across the sheets, seeking his leg. She rolled over voluptuously, in anticipation of the warm obstacle that would stop her. But she rolled, unhindered, all the way to the edge. Nothing prevented her, nothing held. She had the cool expanse entirely to herself. Her husband was no longer there.

He's coming right back, she thought. He'll be here in a heartbeat.

Because maybe he wanted a glass of water, or else drank too many before he went to bed. Maybe he heard footsteps on the stairs, and was waiting, dictionary raised, behind the door. Maybe he was saving them. Maybe he was thirsty. Or maybe, like her, he had fallen in love—with the gypsy queen and her raven hair. The tiny girl tucked inside a tulip. The mermaid, the shield maiden, the daughter crying from the tower. Maybe it was the siren who had called to him. And maybe he had answered, and was gone.

THE BEARS

Once, when I was convalescing, I was sent to a farmhouse in the country. No one there knew I had been sick. A woman came to cook in the evenings, and her daughter would appear at odd hours with a mop and bucket, keeping the place clean. There were many kinds of tea to be found in the kitchen, and a woven tray on which you could arrange the tea things. Also there were deep old wooden chairs lined up along the front porch, so you could sit as long as you liked, looking out over the fields, the trees, and sometimes even the mountains if the sky was truly clear. Because of the porch and the tray and the slow way the day ended, I felt, in this place, though no one knew of my miscarriage, as if I were being gently attended to, as if all the demands of the world had been softly lifted away, and that I should rest.

I had been invited there to finish a chapter on William James. I was to do so in the company of eight other people working on interesting, improbable projects. The invitation had come as a great surprise to me and had a magical effect on my confidence. As soon as I set foot in the farmhouse, however, every thought and hope I had about William James flew out of my head, like bits of charred paper up a chimney. He had been my companion for several months, and now he turned into a man I barely knew. His sudden disappearance made the days seem long. Soon I discovered that the pastimes I had always imagined I'd enjoy—such as dipping into newly published novels, and drifting off to sleep in the middle of the afternoon—left me with a stiff neck, as well as a feeling of dread.

My only relief was in walking along the sides of the highway and the roads. Though they were country roads, they were not laid out in a haphazard way, and I decided that if I was to set out, and turn left, and then left again, turning and turning until I found my way back again, I would be all right. I walked slowly, but for distances that surprised me. I walked without my wallet or my glasses, and my life felt far away. The city I lived in, the appointments I made, the students I taught, my dog, my friend—it seemed as if what held me to them had loosened and let go. When I thought of home, all I remembered was a route I would sometimes follow as I walked to the bus stop, a route that took me past an empty parking lot, where long grasses and weeds had been allowed to grow in profusion. Even though it wasn't strictly on my way, I liked walking past this empty lot because of the wild, sweet smell it sent out into the world. No other lot or overgrown yard I knew of had managed to achieve the right alchemy of grass and clover and tall spindly wildflowers, and no other place could secrete this same smell. But here, along the side of the highway, the smell was everywhere.

Reading the signs that appeared on the road, I learned I was walking through a part of the countryside that had yet to be discovered and made over in a sentimental way. This area remained practical and suspicious. At frequent intervals, sometimes only two or three trees apart, the signs were posted: PRIVATE PROPERTY, they said. Then came a list of numerous activities, followed by the words STRICTLY FORBIDDEN, and for final emphasis, the phrase SHALL BE PROSECUTED. As if these yellow signs left room for doubt and interpretation, some residents had gone to the trouble of making their own: NO VISITORS, said one. NO TRESPASS-ING, said another. And even the cornfields were wrapped around with barbed wire. But not once did I see another person walking along the road. It was hard to imagine who the trespassers might be. Other than me, of course.

The pickup trucks wouldn't slow down when they passed me on the road. They hadn't slowed down for other things either. Along the highway's edge I saw a rabbit, its re-mains vanishing, its bits of fur lifting up from the pavement as dreamily as thistledown; I saw a small black songbird, throbbing with larvae, and a freshly dead chipmunk, curled up on its side as if in sleep. There were also many beauti-ful horses, heraldic and fully alive. I wanted to watch them gallop across the fields with their ravishing black manes streaming behind them, but it seemed when left alone they had little reason to do so. They chose to stand still, in mysterious silence. The cows, in contrast, were full of spirit, but maybe only when being pushed into a trailer. I happened to be walking by while this process was underway. The cows already inside the trailer made an alarming sound, a truly unhappy and outraged sound, the sort of hoarse trumpeting you might hear from an elephant. It could not be described as either mooing or lowing. I wondered where the cows were being taken, whether their misery was mindless and fleeting, as they were simply being driven to another pasture; or whether the truth was darker and the animals sensed the sure approach of death. So I studied the cows, and I noted that these were black, and large, with heavy brows and small eyes, and that their boulder-like bodies hung low to the ground. But what did this mean? I had no idea. I had no way of knowing just where they were off to.

The list of things I did not know was getting longer. I could name only two of the plants that grew in abundance on the side of the road. If there had been a child walking alongside me, its hand in my own, and if this child had shown any curiosity about the world, I would have been able only to say, *That is goldenrod. And that, Queen Anne's lace.* It would have been a poor display of knowledge. Pale starry blue flowers and velvety purses of orange and gold, whole swamps of tawdry purple tapers and creeping vines that spread their fingers out into the road—all of it as common as day, and all of it inscrutable to me. I had also been forced to admit, while trying to write a postcard, that I wasn't completely sure which mountains I was looking at.

The cows, the flowers, the mountain range; why William James had seen fit to abandon me; whether I would ever get well; how to relieve the sorrow of my friend.

That I continued to call him my friend probably added to his unhappiness. But the other names sounded antiseptic to me. Sometimes he would identify himself light-heartedly on phone messages as *the father of your unborn child.* After a certain point, though, this no longer applied. I believed *friend* to be a true honorific, but he said he felt differently, and so what to call him was among the many unknown things that troubled me as I made my slow way around the fields.

But there was always the white house of Jerry Roth, which I did come to know. And, in fact, the house seemed such a reflection of him, I sometimes felt as if I knew him, the man. His house was set back slightly from the road, sitting upon a soft rise in the land; it looked out over the acres of a horse farm, and nearer than that a fishing pond, edged with cattails, shadowed by willow trees, a rowboat resting on its grassy bank. Perfect as in a painting or a dream; as if all the charm and sentiment the countryside had been coolly withholding could now, at last, express itself, could gloriously unfurl in one long exhalation of white clapboard and dappled shade and undulating lawn. A colonial house, but without stiffness or symmetry: a wing rambled off to the right, toward a glassed-in porch, and on the left stood a new addition, a sort of studio or guest quarters, its face yawning open in a wide cathedral window, and its entrance marked by a great glass lantern that echoed, in wittily enormous proportions, the quaint, black-leaded lights that hung beside the front door of the original house.

I did not apprehend all of this graciousness at once. It revealed itself to me in a slow unfolding of surprises. One afternoon, the wind stirred the leaves of Jerry Roth's old maple, and only then did I see how beautifully it spread its canopy across the front lawn, and how thickly the plantings grew beneath it, their dark green leaves polished and aglow, the white flowers floating above their long stems like candle flames. Another day, hearing a window shut, I turned and saw the kaleidoscopic horse standing calmly in the garden. The same size, the same stillness, as the creatures across the road, but its coat glistened with blue sky and yellow stars, with tempera paint and varnish, with winding streams and hills of violet and umber and red. And in this backward glance I also found the apple tree, crooked with age, its lowest branch dipping only a few feet from the ground, extended as if in invitation for a child to take a seat.

What else. There was a plaque attached to the mailbox post, its delicate roman capitals spelling out JEROME ROTH, and beneath that a picture of a pheasant, wings spread, like something you might find on a piece of porcelain. And opposite the mailbox, a square of white-and-blue tin announcing that this little stretch of road should be known as RUE JERRY ROTH (MARIN ÉMÉRITE). The street sign was displayed on a faded red barn, now turned into a garage for three wonderful cars: a wood-paneled station wagon, a Volkswagen van, and a sleek silver two-seater, Japanese and new. One evening, while walking along the highway, I was passed from behind by the wood-paneled station wagon, and my heart quickened involuntarily, as though I'd seen a star.

I guess it shouldn't have surprised me that my heart beat the way it did. For having walked by his house so many times, and gleaned with such pleasure all the small and large details of the world he had made, I admired him. I would have liked him for a friend. Even more, I would have liked him to gather me into his family, a family I imagined as manifesting the same humor and whimsy and discernment that was evident everywhere in his house and on his land. For I knew there must be a family, moving through the clean rooms of the house, laughing and groaning, just beyond the reach of what I could see.

That same evening I returned to the farmhouse, still elated by the sight of the station wagon, to find that there was swordfish for dinner. And tired of my own reticence, I decided I wanted to talk about Jerry Roth. Not to the woman who had cooked the swordfish, with whom I usually talked, but to the people who were eating it with me. I think I would have liked the farmhouse much more if it hadn't been for those eight other people, who would emerge from their rooms at the end of the afternoon, looking dazed and replete. They took turns walking to the village to buy bottles of wine that were opened and poured at dinner. I had to wait for a pause in the conversation; the wine made them talkative, and they had hit again upon a favorite subject: the other farmhouses, castles, villas, and cottages where they had been guests in the past.

Potatoes. At every meal, said Laszlo. Boiled or fried. Or cold, cut up in little chunks and mixed together with a herb I couldn't identify.

But it's Italy! Anna cried.

My point, Laszlo said irritably, and jiggled the wine in his glass. Not what one would expect.

Mary spoke: The first week with the baronessa, I could barely eat, she made me so nervous. And all those little dogs underfoot. I was sure I was going to step on one and cripple it. But the food was good; there were no potatoes.

Ah, so you've been to Santa Maddalena, Laszlo said with a small sigh of resentment.

The platter of swordfish was heaved up into the air and then made its precarious way around the table for a second time.

They are fattening me up here, Cesar said, helping himself.

Haven't you seen that great big oven there in the back? Behind the barn? Erga said. We're going to be plump and delicious when we're done.

She was looking at her plate as she said this, and without eye contact, I could not tell how merrily she intended it. We ate in silence, and for a fleeting moment it seemed possible that we had all been tricked, that this gift of quietude was in fact a term of captivity and terror.

Have you tried walking? I asked them finally. I find that walking helps.

Mary wiped her mouth and gently pushed back her chair.

I just run, she said, I run as fast as I can.

And so it was that I was running the next time I saw the house of Jerry Roth. By that point the running had become painful and strange to me. At first, when I began to run, I felt surprised by my lightness, I felt young and strong, I felt like a child running ecstatically, for no reason at all. But soon that feeling changed and my breath started to disappear. I had to pause to hitch up my jeans and wipe the fog from my glasses. Then, out of perversity, I began running again. Just to that tree, I told myself. And after the tree, an electrical pole, a mailbox, a NO TRESPASSING sign. I kept promising myself that upon reaching these landmarks I would stop, yet I didn't stop, I continued to run, trying to be swift, becoming more damp and anguished as I passed each marker and found another just a little farther on. I must have been bleeding for some time before I noticed it. I suppose I thought the wetness slipping down my legs was sweat. So what made me notice? Maybe the smell, the faint animal smell, a smell that has always made me think of wounded prey in the underbrush, or a mother licking afterbirth off her young. Foolishly, I had not been expecting it. In the deepest part of me, I had not believed that my body would return to normal, or that one day I would be well again.

I'm not sure if it was the thought of being well or the memory of getting sick that affected me. But either way, I bent over and started to cry. For the first time I wanted help, but predictably no one was near; there was a detached humming in the air, coming from the hidden insects or the electrical lines overhead. The horses and cows were absent from the fields. The sun burned indistinctly behind a thin screen of clouds. I limped out to the middle of the road, but I couldn't see any trucks in the distance, approaching me at dangerous speeds. I was at a loss. I didn't even know what to call the place where I had stopped. There was a route number posted on a sign a few hundred yards ahead, but that number had no meaning for me.

Standing there in the road, I was visited by an idea, startling and clear. It was the idea of crisis; the idea that I was in the midst of having one. And with this idea, my earlier sense of lightness returned, and though my face was burning and my chest hurt and sharp pains were rocketing up my shins, I wanted to run again. I wanted to get there fast. For I knew now exactly where I was going.

I knew, too, what I was going to tell him. Why I had come, a stranger running down the road, and knocked on his door. Doubled over on the threshold of his old house, beneath the black-leaded lights, breathless and red-faced, dark stains growing on the legs of my pants. And it wasn't completely untrue. It had been true only two months before, but then I had been in the restroom on the third floor of my department, inside a stall where the metal was beginning to show through the gray-green paint, as a slender graduate student I had once taught was energetically brushing her teeth at the sink. She had probably just finished eating one of the frugal, grainy meals she brought with her to campus in a cloudy plastic container.

So I ran as best as I could until at last the white house

appeared before me; I climbed the steps at the base of the slope, followed the flagstone path, passed beneath the branches of the magnificent tree, all the while ushered along by the profound sense of permission that the word *crisis* had given me. In fact I'd come to feel that I was seeking help for someone other than myself. As if under a spell, I lifted the knocker, and when the brass hammer dropped down on its plate, the force of its fall eased open the door, which was, of course, unlocked. Jerry Roth shared none of his neighbors' suspicions. No bolts, no barbed wire, just a half-lit entryway with a good Turkish carpet and a bowl of summer roses, and beyond that a bright kitchen smelling of coffee and slightly burnt toast. And the table! The table was even better than I'd imagined: huge, rough-hewn, radiant with age, practically seaworthy; surely salvaged from a tumbledown farm nearby and then refurbished at some expense. The kitchen chairs looked rescued too, mismatched as they were, some with spindles, others slatted, one with a little painting of grapes and fruits fading on its back, all of them gathered in expectation around the table, as charming and different as children. The chair I sat in had narrow armrests, and I could feel the shallow dip in the wood where hundreds of other elbows had rested, or maybe only a few chosen elbows repeatedly over the course of a hundred years. The newspaper was close at hand, not the local paper but the *Times*, whose presence I so missed that I almost started crying again, already opened to the film section, my favorite, and a review of an Iranian movie that my friend and I planned to see together.

The review was admiring, not to anyone's surprise, and full of the sort of empty reverential phrases—*a master of world cinema*, etc.—that made my friend particularly impatient. My friend had little patience with a number of things: dog owners, pigeons, overcooked food, fatuous reviews, ATM fees, antiques, and people's mispronunciation of his name. Yet he had been unfailingly patient with me. Opening the windows wide, reading to me from William James, walking my dog, taking my clothes and sheets to the laundromat. Why something that not only ended but began in an accident should have so undone me—but, well, it did. And he had been undone too, which moved me. It made me realize that he'd been serious all along.

As I was finishing the review, an orange cat wandered into the kitchen and promptly jumped up onto the table, and for the first time I experienced a pang of disapproval: Jerry Roth was not a great disciplinarian with his animals, and the cat settled itself right on top of the newspapers. I moved a dish out of the way so the cat wouldn't lick the butter from the toast, deciding as I did so that I might as well eat the rest of the toast myself, since it was already cold.

Did I call out at any point? Make myself known? I think I said hello when I stepped inside his house; I must have done that. But I felt quite sure, quite quickly, that no one was home, despite the cups and dishes still scattered on the table, despite the smell of breakfast in the air. The house had the quality of being recently and hurriedly evacuated, but not for any sinister reason—maybe the kids were late for swim practice, or the milk had run out. They had left the house in a rush; they would be back soon; but for now, it was mine.

All my senses opened in recognition. The mixed scent of newsprint and butter, the muted ticking of the modern cuckoo clock on the wall, the enamel teakettle gleaming atop the immense stove, the marmalade still sharp in my mouth: home. Here it was. Or something like it. Something homelike. *Heimlich.* How would the Germans say it? *Gemütlich.* Touchingly, where the soul or spirit belongs. To put it another way, cozy. Which did not describe my overheated apartment in the city, or the dim, chaotic ranch house I'd grown up in, places that were home but not home, not the home I wished to have, might one day have, if time or means or aptitude ever allowed it. A home I'd have to make. Sitting at Jerry Roth's table, I felt suddenly that I'd spent my adult life engaged in the most impoverished kind of making. What did I have to show but lecture notes, a short book on other books, comments in the margins of seminar papers, an occasional terrarium? It occurred to me then that to make a kitchen like this required a breadth of imagination I might not be able to summon.

Back at the farmhouse there was a pedestal in the corner of the sitting room, and on the pedestal sat a large guest book that held the names of past visitors, a book I had already leafed through many times, trying to kill the afternoon. Most of the names meant little to me, but once in a while a name would leap out from the page and spread its light over the room—a moment both exhilarating and deeply shameful for me as I was reminded that I had no business being there. The guest book adhered to a formula, full name followed by discipline and date of residency, and one of the earlier entries stopped me, because instead of putting down *architect* or *composer* or *essayist*, the visitor had written, in slim capital letters, *HOMEMAKER*. But she was a poet, I knew—a poet of such importance that even I, who almost never read poetry, perked up at the sight of her name. She had written this in 1976, long enough ago that it was hard for me to interpret her use of the word. Was it a political act to write that, a reclamation? A gesture of defiance? Or could it be modesty. Self-doubt. A wry critique of taxonomy and titles? Maybe, more simply, she felt it the most apt description of how she spent her days. I couldn't tell; though the writing itself looked black and fresh, her intent remained distant and unreadable to me. Nevertheless this entry in the guest book made me happy. In the years since she wrote it, her genius as a poet had been named and rewarded, and I liked how the word she chose early for herself now had the glamour of genius attached to it; how *HOMEMAKER* reached forward through time and lightly claimed that.

The orange cat shifted peaceably on the newspaper. I considered fixing myself another piece of toast, or finding a guest room and lying down to rest for a few minutes. My body was still tired and weird from all the running, and when I stood up from my chair, my knees buckled and I nearly lost my balance. I laid my palm on the knotted surface of the table. Through the wide kitchen windows I could see the rainbow horse waiting in the garden, and beyond that, the crooked apple tree. A fringe of young trees grew along the property line, weakly shielding the back lawn from the shaggier woods that rose up behind them, and while I was staring at the saplings, trying to figure out what kind they were, I saw a large body emerge from the forest and start lumbering toward the house. It took me a second to realize that the body belonged to a man. It was so pale and slow and enormous, and wearing such a short and colorful bathrobe, I thought unfairly at first that I must be seeing a woman, a morbidly obese woman in a swimming cap. But what I mistook for a swimming cap was actually a bald head. And as the man drew closer, I understood more and more clearly the size of him. He moved laboriously, shuffling more than walking, halting every few steps to catch his breath. His head shone and his shoulders heaved. The hem of his bathrobe fluttered above legs that looked at once curdled and bloated, swollen to the point of bursting. His leg flesh drooped over his knees.

I knew but did not accept that this man approaching the house was Jerry Roth. He made his slow, huffing way across the lawn in the unconscious manner of someone who had done so a thousand times before. Upon noticing something in the grass, he kicked at it briefly, but didn't, probably couldn't, bend over to pick it up. It seemed impossible that the man responsible for this house was the same as the huge, repellent person kicking at his lawn.

Jerry Roth then lifted his eyes and blindly took in the whole of his house, or at least the back view of it, a view I had never seen, and I must have forgotten that I was as fully apparent to him as he was to me, because I continued to gaze at my ease from the kitchen, and felt truly shocked when his blank stare narrowed into a hard look, pointed in my direction like a gun. He stopped short and raised a heavy arm to block the sun's glare from his eyes. I could see now that his bright bathrobe was covered in flocks of flying cranes, wings and necks outstretched. Suddenly he dropped his arm and began moving toward me at a pace I didn't think possible for him.

In that moment I thought meaningfully, for the first time in several weeks, about William James; in this case, about William James and his bear. To explain, James published an influential paper in 1884, a paper titled "What Is an Emotion?," and in this paper James put forth the theory that standard emotions such as sadness or rage or fear are not antecedent to the physiological responses we associate with them, but rather the product of these bodily changes. This was a radical notion at the time, a reversal of the usual way of seeing things. Common sense, according to James, tells us that when we lose our fortune, we are sorry and weep; we meet a bear, are frightened and run; we are insulted by a rival, are angry and strike. Yet this order of sequence is incorrect, James asserted: The more rational statement is that we feel sorry because we cry; angry because we strike, afraid because we tremble. Coming between the stimulus (bear) and the feeling (fear) is the body: quickened heartbeat, shallow breathing, trembling lips, weakened limbs. And that collection of responses is what lets you know that you're afraid.

My own research had very little to do with his theory of emotion, and I confess to feeling somewhat irritated when the bear would be brought up almost immediately upon my mentioning an interest in William James. Why did it loom so large in people's memory, and why did it seem to be the only aspect of James's work that they retained? It needled me, enough so that at some point I went back and reread the paper, only to discover that the famous bear made the most minor of appearances, invoked only twice and amid a series of instances. Much more remarkable to me was the story James tells of being a child of seven or eight years old and seeing a horse bled. The blood was in a bucket, with a stick in it; James stirred the blood around and, his childish curiosity aroused, lifted the stick to watch the blood drip from it. Then, without warning, he fell over in a dead faint. James recalls feeling, even at such a young age, astonished that the mere presence of a pailful of red liquid could provoke *such formidable bodily effects*. The child and his bucket of blood—now why didn't anyone remember that?

But as I stood there frozen in the kitchen of Jerry Roth's house, I felt in my every muscle the indelibleness of James's oft-cited example. It was simple. When you meet a bear in the woods, you run. And of course that is what I did: I ran.

In another version of the story, I jump out the nearest window and break my neck in the fall. Otherwise I am devoured, or thrown into a fire, or drowned. Barring that, I am dropped from a church steeple as punishment. In the version first recorded by Robert Southey, I manage to get away but am taken up by the constable and sent to the House of Corrections for being the vagrant that I am. It takes almost no effort to dig up these variations; over time, the trespasser turns from curious fox to bad old woman to bold little girl: a girl who is at the start called Silver Hair but who eventually gets saddled with the cloying name she hasn't been able to shake since. Given the possibilities, it's clearly best to be young, blond, and impertinent, because then you do not suffer any retribution for what you've done. Your escape is assured. As for me, I am over thirty-five, soft-spoken, brown-skinned—yet I, too, seem to have gotten off scot-free.

It can be difficult, however, to sift out retribution from reward, to really tell the two apart, commingled as they often are. For instance, after I left the farmhouse, having never touched my chapter on William James, my friend and I decided to have another go at it, this time more solemnly and deliberately than before, and to our indescribable relief, it stuck. My body grew larger and larger, unrecognizably larger, until suddenly one morning our daughter was born. We rigged up a sort of three-sided crib at the edge of the bed that allowed me to reach for her in the middle of the night and to nurse, without ever having to sit up or even raise my head from the pillow, and when she was done, I'd just slide her back on her special shelf and fall asleep again. Which is all to say that though she slept beside me I never worried, in those blurry months, about rolling over on my child and smothering her; among the many possible horrors I worried over, this was not one of them, this was one of the few I could lay to rest. Strangely, though, my body remained convinced that I had to stay very still as I was sleeping, that I couldn't toss about or sprawl, that I needed to contain myself to a sliver of the bed, as if to avoid the risk of something terrible happening. It was an odd compulsion, and my hand or arm would often go numb as the result of sleeping in this anxious, unmoving way. Then one night my daughter's voice punctured my dreaming so cleanly that I was able to hold the shape of the dream before it vanished, and its shape was the shape of Jerry Roth, the monstrous bulk of him, heaving softly beside me in the bed, and I knew, I knew, that I couldn't move, because to wake him would be—to what? To die? My heart raced, my breath was shallow. I brought my hands to my chest and they were damp with sweat. In the darkness this felt like fear. But I lifted the elastic band on my underwear and put a hand between my legs, and I understood then that my rigid, dreaming body hadn't been afraid. After wiping my fingers on the sheets, I reached out and found my daughter on her shelf.

As if not to be stopped, I became pregnant again, sooner than expected, and the apartment soon revealed itself as too expensive and too small, making the once unimaginable choice appear to us natural, attractive, inescapable, imminent: we moved to a house in the country. Our town is less than two hours away from the city by train; the backyards peter out into forests or fields; the houses are for the most part run-down, but with a lot of original detail, as the agent liked to say. A specialty food shop has bravely opened up, and there is a drive-in movie theater that still operates in the summer. At dusk, we flick the insects from our eyes and turn blankly to the wide, transparent sky, something like calm sliding over us.

But the days can be long, which I remember from my first stay in the country, and I often catch myself calculating the hours and little activities until dusk falls and the train comes in and the babies are put to sleep. The stretch between the morning nap and the afternoon nap always has a particular endlessness to it. My children are just different enough in age to be impossible to entertain simultaneously; what mesmerizes one infuriates the other; their developmental stages appear mortally opposed. I shuttle between the two of them to neither's satisfaction. Like a bad employee I tend to hang back and dawdle, taking longer than necessary in the bathroom, surreptitiously checking my email, drawn helplessly to any window to watch the smooth, indifferent functioning of the seductive world outside. There's usually not that much to see. A couple of guys from the power company checking the lines, or the older husband and wife from down the road, walking in single file and not talking, intent on their exercise. The mailman, of course; or in our case, the mailwoman. More rarely, the brown UPS truck. But every once in a while I'll look out the window and see someone who doesn't belong there, like an overweight girl wearing enormous headphones and jogging miserably, or a woman dressed in city clothes who tramps along the side of the road with a faint frown on her face. I have no way of knowing who she is and where she's off to, but she looks so unlikely out there among the gravel and the weeds, and so impractically dressed, that I briefly wonder if her car has broken down. I think to open the door and call out to her, asking if she needs help, if everything's all right, but to do so seems altogether impossible, as impossible as one of those huge prehistoric fish half hibernating at the bottom of the tank knocking on the glass and mouthing *hello!* to a bright, quickly moving visitor on the other side. To our mutual embarrassment, though, she sees me, our eyes meet, and after automatically glancing away she looks back at me again and lifts her hand in a tentative wave. I wave back at her, electrified and sad. And then my daughter, in the far distance somewhere, lets out a long howl of frustration, and by the time I've gotten down on my hands and knees, rescued the wooden mixing spoon from under the stove, rinsed it off in hot water, hurried back to the window—the woman walking down the highway has already moved on, innocent of what waits for her, and passed out of sight.

MANY A LITTLE MAKES

Mickle. I hope I'm texting you at the right number. I tried sending you a message on FB but it seems you don't go on there anymore. Good for you! I keep meaning to close down my account but then I see a photo of someone's kid at a march and I get sucked in again. Speaking of which LOVED the video of Rose's cello recital. I know it was from last year but literal tears when I saw it bc of listening to Bach suites with you when we couldn't fall asleep remember?

Rose is such a beautiful poised creative young woman and I just wish the kids could meet her they would love each other. They are all so big I can't believe it. Life out here agrees with them but the bus can feel very small at times and especially when they're fighting hahahaha. Bark beetles continue to decimate in nightmarish fashion but silver lining my study has been extended six months. Big hole in the canopy now sadly and so much more light coming through so collecting new data on red squirrels and snowshoe hares. Kids complain my hands always smell like peanut butter!!! I tell them not bad as far as occupational hazards go.

Jon busy doing online portion of reiki certification and fingers crossed will get license when we go home next year. Strange to write that bc here has started to feel like home and I am tbh kind of dreading going back. Quite amazing the resources out there for people in our boat (hahaha BUS). Homeschooling community . . . wow! Impassioned. Kids are learning Japanese! They wrote a tanks about blue spruce I want to show your mother. TANKA sorry clearly phone doesn't speak Japanese

The texts arrived from a number Mari didn't recognize. Even the area code was unknown to her, and it didn't help that she thumbed through the messages backward, in reverse order. But there were only two people in the world who called her by that name, and Imogen's various phone numbers (N.Y. cell, D.C. cell, office, home) were already saved in her contacts. So it had to be Bree.

In the sixth grade, on the subject of Bree, Mari's mother had this to say: *Three can get complicated.* She was talking about the dynamics of female friendship, a topic that Mari did not relish discussing. In general she found her mother's warnings reliably wrong but also impossible to forget, like shampoo slogans or the songs sung at camp. When, one Friday afternoon in November, she discovered herself lodged between Imogen and Bree in the back seat of a car heading swiftly to the mall, this earworm wriggled up to the surface and she thought at her mother: HA.

They were fine.

A thin stream of air flowed over them, and the radio played a song they knew most of the words to. Bree was saying that they should buy their tickets before they got food in case the movie sold out, and Imogen was saying that a dog waiting at the corner to cross looked a lot like a larger, fluffier version of her dog, Hamish. They all craned their heads to look at the dog. Mari could jump in at any moment with a funny or pointless comment if it occurred to her, but if it didn't, she didn't have to say anything at all.

Imogen had befriended Mari at the beginning of second grade, back when Mari was the only new girl in the class. Years passed and then Bree arrived, along with an assortment of other sixth-grade girls. Out of all of them Imogen chose Bree, for reasons not obvious to Mari. Bree wore eyeglasses with tinted plastic arms that swooped downward in a secretarial way. She had short brown hair and the long, waistless torso of a dachshund. On the first day of school, she appeared in a teal sweatshirt violently spattered with paint, a top that Mrs. Schmidt said was jazzy. It looked store-bought, not homemade, like something she had saved up for.

Bree took the trolley to school from a town called Revere with the help of a student transportation pass that hung from a lanyard around her neck, which she removed every morning and tucked carefully in her book bag as she was entering the building. In the locker room, Mari had overheard some girls pronouncing Revere as "Ruh-vee-ah" in order to amuse each other, and this was how she learned that Revere was an undesirable place, inhabited by locals who couldn't tell how thick their accents were. But Bree didn't say it that way; she spoke quickly and correctly and without any accent at all, participating in class with palpable happiness no matter what the subject was. She was "bright," Mari saw early on, which was probably what made her interesting to Imogen. Any girl at their school was smart enough to be there, or at least well-organized, but not many of them, not even a few of them, had an air of intensity.

To be clear, Bree wasn't excessively studious or preoccupied with cerebral pursuits, and Imogen and Mari weren't, either. They didn't read Russian novels or follow current events or dismantle electronics to figure out how they worked. Together they circled the mall and talked about their teachers and occasionally stopped to go inside a store and touch things that they wanted to buy. They ate swirled frozen yogurt and then watched a blockbuster movie full of French kissing and shoot-outs. But if, for instance, the sight of a botanical rendering of lavender wrapped around a bar of soap should suddenly fill Mari with a rich, heady, Eleanor of Aquitaine feeling, and if later she went home and pulled off the cookbook shelf an illustrated guide to medieval herbs from which she painstakingly copied out on little sheets of paper the properties and uses of yarrow, chamomile, mugwort, and horehound, and then dipped the sheets of paper in tea and dried them outside so as to make them look more like parchment, neither Imogen nor Bree would wonder at it. Not that they would ever do the same; they weren't excited by herbs. It's just that they would recognize, wordlessly, the impulse to do so.

That's what the three of them had in common. Otherwise, Mari and Bree were short while Imogen was tall. Imogen and Bree were white and Mari was Japanese. Bree lived in Revere and Imogen and Mari did not. Their differences were evenly distributed, yet when Mari glimpsed a reflection of them gliding past a department store's plate-glass window, she saw with perfect clarity that Imogen belonged to another species altogether, like a wood elf among dwarves, or a human escorting hobbits. Her hair shone in the muted light pouring down through the atrium. Her shoulders were pulled back, and her neck was long. When she laughed, she opened her mouth wide and you could see practically every one of her straight, gleaming teeth. She didn't have a single cavity. However sometimes her breath up close could smell a little bit sour, a detail you'd have to be her best friend to know, because to the rest of the world she was just a radiant creature passing by, laughing, her head floating well above the other two.

What did they talk about?

"They're making us do the mile-run next week."

"Who told you?"

"Coach Bell."

"I love Coach Bell. I wish we had her more often."

"I can't do it. I will die. I will collapse from exhaustion, and then they'll try to revive me on the side of the field and realize I'm dead."

"What if we walk? Like speed walk? Or jog very slowly and then walk?"

"Last year I tried that but Coach Boudreau threatened me and said she'd make me do the whole mile over again if I didn't start moving."

" 'Moving with *a greater sense of urgency.*' "

"That's why you guys always say that?"

"*She* got the second-fastest time in the grade. And she had a cold."

"Shannon was so much faster than me, it wasn't even close."

"I don't like being timed. It makes me feel like a race-horse."

"I'm more like a cow. Cows move at their own pace."

"We should tell them we're cows and that running is not in our nature."

"Running for a *mile*. That's dangerous for a cow."

"Don't say that. You're not cows. You're more graceful than cows."

And so on.

Mari hadn't had a new friend in so long that she had almost forgotten what it was like to go to someone's house for the first time, the inevitable shock to the senses. The smell most of all, not unpleasant but unfamiliar. The school year was nearly finished before Bree invited them over, and it turned out that she lived on the right side of a graying clapboard house that had an identical left side where a different family lived. A flight of concrete stairs rose from the sidewalk, and at its top was a shallow concrete porch, and there on either side stood two front doors, exactly symmetrical even down to their storm-door handles, which meant that one door opened up to the left and the other one to the right. Squashed behind the storm door on the left was a scarecrow holding a sign that said WELCOME in autumn colors. "We don't talk to them anymore," Bree whispered as she extracted her lanyard, which in addition to her trolley pass held her house keys. "Long story."

She opened the door and out leapt the smell of her house, indefinable but strong, a little reminiscent of chicken noodle soup in a can. Soon enough it went away. Bree had cable TV, tropical fish, and a toilet lid covered in burgundy carpet. The three of them bargained over which channel they would watch, and somehow it felt easier to be flexible and magnanimous when more than one other party was involved in the negotiations. As they were eating cereal and watching music videos, Bree's mother appeared, holding her younger sister by the hand, and while Bree's mother looked about the right age for Bevin, who was four, she didn't look like she belonged to Bree, despite having a lot of the same soft, unformed features. With her ponytail and scuffed-up sneakers, she looked more like a big sister, like the eldest in a family of sisters fending for themselves after their parents had died in a tragic car accident. Or maybe Mari's and Imogen's parents were simply old. Mari couldn't recall seeing any of them wearing tennis shoes while not playing tennis. "Make yourself at home, girls," Bree's mother said to them with strange formality, and ushered Bevin upstairs for a bath.

Darkness fell, and Bree suggested baking a cake. She made it sound like the idea had only just occurred to her, but in the kitchen she pulled out the bowl and the hand mixer and the measuring cups and the cake mix from a single cabinet, all ready to go, and Mari filled suddenly with so much tenderness that her eyes watered. The mix was Duncan Hines and the flavor was, mysteriously, "yellow." At Mari's house, what passed for cake was a nearly flavorless sponge that her mother bought at the Japanese bakery and then urged guests to try, assuring them that it was "very light" and "not too sweet." When Bree dumped the yellow mix into the bowl, it sent up a mushroom cloud of synthetic sugariness that caused Mari to choke. Imogen was perched on the counter and slicing a plastic spatula through the air, as if felling enemies. She didn't try to contribute anything. She looked on good-naturedly as Mari and Bree followed the box's directions, and once the cake pans, trembling with batter, were slid into the oven, she held out her arms to receive the empty mixing bowl.

"Oh nice," she said. "You left a lot on the sides." Without hesitating she sank her spatula into the bowl, circled it around, lifted it back up, and inserted its entire drippy width into her mouth. It came out clean. "Share," Bree said. Imogen scraped the bowl again and Mari watched the slathered spatula head disappear inside Bree's open mouth.

The third time Imogen dipped into the bowl, she presented the mouthful of batter to Mari.

"No thanks," Mari said lightly, and drew back from the spatula. She deliberately did not say what she wanted to say, what was foremost in her mind, what was exactly the thing her mother had spoken ominously of: *salmonella*. Because her mother was usually wrong. Her mother, for instance, had assumed that just because Bree was eight years older than her sister there had to be "different fathers," as she put it. Something about the tactful tone she used made Mari want to strangle her. "It's the same dad," Mari had announced in a clipped voice, "and don't worry, him and her mom are *married*. And yes, she will be at home the whole time we're there."

"*He* and her mom," her own mother had answered, at which point Mari had covered her ears and let out a moan.

Yet three large eggs had plopped glisteningly into that batter, three large raw eggs probably teeming with bacteria, and just the sight of its yellowness slicking the spatula was making Mari feel queasy. That, and the sickly sweet smell. And the buzzy fluorescent lights in Bree's kitchen. And all the saliva being passed around freely.

By now her friends were looking at each other and smiling. They'd seen right through her airy demurral. Pantherlike, Imogen hopped down from the counter while Bree closed in on Mari from the other side.

"Just try some," Imogen murmured. "You'll like it."

She handed the spatula off to Bree but held on to the

bowl, dragging the length of her finger along its interior and then extracting it, coated. She slid the finger into her mouth.

"It's the best part." Bree swam the spatula closer to Mari's face. "Trust us. It's delicious."

"I don't want to," Mari said from under the collar of her T-shirt, which she'd pulled up over her nose.

"Just a little," Imogen said. "Just a little tiny taste." Bree stuck out her tongue and delicately pressed the spatula to its tip. "See?" Imogen continued. "It'll be that tiny. You'll barely taste it."

Mouth ajar, Bree darted her tongue in and out, in and out, in and out, very fast. Where did she learn to do that? It looked disturbing, like in a Prince kind of way. The yellow droplet sat at the end of her flickering tongue. Mari twisted her head aside.

"You're pressuring me." Her voice was muffled beneath the T-shirt. "I don't like eating batter or being pressured or throwing up all night and getting hospitalized."

"Who said anything about throwing up?"

She yanked her shirt back down and glared at them. "Hello—salmonella?"

Somehow it sounded less insane when her mother said it. Imogen and Bree stared at her, speechless. Then they both cackled. "Salmonella?" they repeated. "Salmonella?" Their eyes glittered. A look of silent understanding passed among the three of them. There was no averting what was coming next.

With a gasp, Mari shoved past Imogen and dove toward the TV room. They flew after her, unleashed, made swift by their socks on the linoleum. Over and around the leather sectional they chased her, careful to avoid the glowing fish tank, no one shrieking or laughing because upstairs Bevin was already asleep. Just their heavy breathing filled the room, and when the two of them finally pinned her to the floor, she could feel how all of their chests were heaving rapidly, in unison, like they had run a mile together with matching strides.

Chariots of Fire was one of her top-five favorite films. Though she didn't like to run herself, the sight of British men running was very moving. Whenever they sang "Jerusalem" in morning meeting, she and Imogen and Bree would entertain themselves by surreptitiously acting out the words; they would mime the seizing of the bow, and the spear, and the countenance divine shining forth upon the hills, and they would attack the low note in "arrows of de-*sire*" with fake solemnity, but even as they joked around, Mari found the song unspeakably beautiful. That ardent phrase—"Bring me my chariot of fire!"—stirred her.

When it touched her face, the cake batter was not cold, as she thought it might be; it felt only thick and wet. Her eyes were closed at this point. And her mouth too, of course. Nothing—not Duncan Hines, or egg-borne bacteria, or anything not her own—would cross the threshold. Her lips were squeezed so tightly shut that they tingled. No one was getting in or out: she kept herself intact, impervious to the panting weight of Imogen and Bree on top of her. With satisfaction, she felt their bodies slacken, the energy dissolving—they were thwarted, and there was nothing to do now but smear batter on Mari's face. Even with her eyes shut, she could tell when it was Imogen doing it and when it was Bree. Like in *Chariots of Fire*, where the two men ran extremely fast but for different reasons: the Scottish one because he believed so much in God, the Jewish one because he wanted to fit in and show that he was better than all the anti-Semites he met in college. The perfunctory swipes across her cheek—that was Imogen, having already lost interest in the whole thing—but in the precisely centered dabs on her forehead, her nose, her mouth, her chin, she felt the warmth of Bree's attention, her thoroughness and care.

After they hoisted themselves off her, Mari made her way unsteadily toward the hall bathroom, eyes slitted and face sticky, and it was here that she caught a whiff of the cake baking in the oven. She had never smelled anything like it before. Initially it reminded her of the cloying scent of Play-Doh, which she had always hated, and in fact hated so much that when small she'd refused to touch the stuff, but as she inhaled again she found something spreading underneath the sweetness, a smell similar to that of butter and eggs and vanilla and flour but not quite the real thing, a smell that was artificial but also intoxicating and somehow more intoxicating for being fake. She didn't have to taste it to know ahead of time how much she was going to like this cake. How moist it would be, and warm, how its faint chemical aftertaste would make her go back for more. Wiping off her face above the sink, she decided to tell her mother that from now on the only kind of cake she wanted for her birthday was yellow cake from a box.

———

In the middle of seventh grade, Mari heard the Smiths for the first time, on a late-night radio show that played the day's most requested songs. She had to spend extra money when buying their record because it was imported from the U.K.; it had a Dutch-blue cover with a black-and-white photograph on it of a handsome man in profile, in a tank top—a man who turned out not to be one of the Smiths, despite a superficial resemblance to their bass player. Printed tinily on the inside record sleeve was every word to every song, which was how she learned that the correct words were *I am the son and the heir* and not *I am the sun and the air*, as she'd originally thought. At first she felt unsophisticated for having heard it this way, but then it occurred to her that maybe the ambiguity was deliberate, a mark of genius.

Once she bought the record, the Smiths became the most important part of Mari's life. She made friends with a girl in her class named Melanie because Melanie was the only other person she knew who'd heard of them. For Mari's birthday, Melanie wrote a pretend letter in which Johnny Marr, the guitarist, declared his love for her, and though Mari put the letter in her treasure box, she didn't plan on rereading it. Speaking as herself, Melanie pointed out that the similarity between Mari's first name and Johnny's last name couldn't be entirely coincidence.

Imogen and Bree didn't have strong feelings either way about the Smiths—Imogen liked soft rock with soaring choruses, and Bree listened to the kind of dance music played on Kiss 108—but still they were Mari's best friends. She went back and forth between trying to convert Imogen and Bree to her excellent tastes and wanting to keep the Smiths as something sacredly her own. But how could you help but share that which took up so much space in your mind? She talked about them daily, and though her friends wouldn't necessarily know a Smiths song if it hit them over the head, they could recite the names and instruments of the band members, and could recognize them in photos; they now knew that Manchester was a city not only in New Hampshire but also in Northern England, that there was nothing Morrissey relished more than going to a stationery shop and sniffing envelopes. They trailed behind Mari and took turns carrying her book bag as she drifted down the dim aisles, inhaling, grazing the reams of paper with her fingertips, attempting through her senses to transport her soul elsewhere.

When that didn't work, they went across the street to get pizza. Each of them could order automatically for the others: Bree always got sausage and mushroom with a medium-size Sprite. Imogen liked Hawaiian, her favorite meat product being Canadian bacon, but Dino's didn't offer that by the slice; you had to order a whole pizza. For just a slice, she'd take pepperoni, as long as there wasn't too much oil pooling in the pepperoni cups. Mari had stopped eating animals of late and wanted only two cheese slices and a free cup of water. Without needing to confer, they headed to the booth in the back corner so that Bree could gaze up at the wood-veneer wall and enjoy the signed photograph of the baseball player who looked like Bruce

Boxleitner, star of *Scarecrow and Mrs. King.* That was her favorite show, just as Imogen's was *Jeopardy!*, just as Mari's was *Masterpiece Theatre.*

The facts in which they were fluent could fill a three-drawer file cabinet: age at which ears were pierced; history of broken bones and origins of scars; score on most recent math test; recurring bad dream; favorite words in French; despised body parts; last book read; secret sources of pride; pet peeves; pet names; scents of deodorant and hair conditioner.

There were also things about each other that they didn't know.

For example: Mari got her period in the sixth grade, right before she turned twelve. By the time she exited the bathroom—sobered, walking strangely, feeling diapered—her mother had already placed calls to her father (he was at work) and both of her grandmothers (California, Ohio) to tell them the news. From that moment forward, Mari never spoke of her period to anyone. Discreetly, she carried the necessary implements in an unassuming cotton pouch made to look like a mouse. She had found it in the top drawer of her mother's dresser, a home to scarves and handkerchiefs and the occasional purposeless gift from relatives abroad. It was an abstract, teardrop-shaped mouse, with a few inches of silk cord extending from its bottom and where the tip of its nose would be, a single snap. With this snap as the only form of closure on an otherwise openmouthed mouse, the pouch was not capable of safely holding much—not money or makeup and certainly not jewelry, nothing small. But Mari discovered that it did well enough with pads, and in fact the pads made the mouse look plump, almost like a stuffed toy, and soon the sight of it nestled in her book bag ceased to cause her any embarrassment, so that eventually, a year later, when she had graduated to tampons, she kept these along with her pads inside the same mouse, which by then had lost its tail.

One winter afternoon, as the seventh graders were packing up their binders in the final minutes before the bell rang, Mari's book bag tipped over onto the floor, and the force of the fall sent the tailless mouse sailing out of her bag like a missile, nose first, and a single slender-size tampon came shooting out of the mouse's open mouth. It was like one of those fireworks that explodes only to reveal that there's another, smaller explosion right inside it. The tampon slid across the homeroom floor without resistance, and Mari watched its journey in frozen horror. It didn't make the slightest difference that only girls went to her school. Girls in her class thought that periods were disgusting: see how someone had tortured Holly Maynard by leaving a used-looking pad, colored red with a felt-tip marker, on the seat of her chair.

Yet three rows ahead of Mari was Bree's solid dachshund body, which happened to be bending down patiently to retrieve a highlighter from beneath her desk just as Mari's tampon came gliding toward her; she scooped it up, tucked it inside the sleeve of her sweatshirt, and sat back up without glancing around to see where it might have come from. Mari dropped onto her knees to recapture the mouse, and Bree bent over again to pick up the highlighter for real, and there among the legs of chairs and desks and classmates their eyes met. Nodding at the cotton pouch clutched in her hand, Bree mouthed to Mari, "I have it."

After the last bell they found themselves laughing uncontrollably in the empty restroom across from the admissions office. Bree had Mari's tampon—and she also had her period—not right then but in life—and she also had gotten hers the year before. In February. Only weeks after Mari. How could they be such complete and utter idiots? Their laughter made them hold on to each other for balance. "Remember when I said that the gyros from lunch were giving me a stomachache?" Bree asked. "That was cramps!" Mari was laughing so hard she couldn't breathe. To think that they had been suffering silently, side by side, this whole time: it felt like both the saddest and funniest thing that had ever happened to them. As she wiped her eyes on her sweatshirt, Bree asked, "Are we going to tell Imogen?" but before she had even finished the question she was already saying, at the same time as Mari, "No."

It was hard to imagine Imogen having bodily functions. Of course they had on countless occasions heard her peeing in the next stall over, but the girl who emerged a few seconds later appeared not responsible for the sounds. Her bathroom at home was spotless: on the sink sat a cake of soap, a boar-bristle brush, a tube of baking soda toothpaste. The porcelain had a lovely soft look to it due to age and abrasive cleaners. A tarnished silver baby cup held Imogen's toothbrush, and though it looked like an antique from the Victorian era, like something you'd find inside a glass case, she used it every morning and night when brushing her teeth. On its rim was a pale crescent of mineral residue.

Imogen's house was full of such objects. There was a low-slung leather rhinoceros, long enough to sit on, with *Liberty of London* stamped on the underside of its ear. There was a needlepoint sampler hanging on the wall that said: *Children aren't happy with nothing to ignore / And that's what parents were created for.* There was a collection of Edward Gorey books—not the big paperback compilations that Mari owned, but original editions, of varying small sizes, with jewel-colored book jackets—*The Doubtful Guest, The Hapless Child, The Epileptic Bicycle, The Glorious Nosebleed.* There was a zither and a tabla. A hand-carved bellows beside the fireplace. Dark blue candles, in pewter candlesticks, that were lit every night at dinner. Also a candle snuffer.

Suffusing everything was the faded smell of woodsmoke from the fireplace, and the stronger smell of eucalyptus branches in earthenware jugs. On top of that, when he came in wet from outside, the musty smell of Hamish.

Hamish was Imogen's cairn terrier, and she also had a brother named Nicholas. He was older than Imogen by four years. He was large and shaggy and beautiful, not an athlete but the co-captain of the debate team at his school. For Mari, who didn't have siblings, his presence was slightly stupefying. If they encountered each other in the kitchen, he would greet her with an electric smile and a booming

"Hey you!" but then have nothing more to say. They would go about their business in cordial silence. Wanting to feel like Johnny Marr, she once asked Nicholas if he would show her how to play a chord on his guitar, and after a strenuous minute of wrestling her hand into position, he finally said, "Huh. You've kind of got stubby fingers, don't you."

When Bree first became friends with them, she was unrestrained on the subject of Nicholas. She embarrassed both Imogen and Mari by acting ridiculous as soon as he left the room: shaking her head in disbelief, fanning her face with her hand. Eventually she caught on and cut it out, or at least she stopped doing it in front of them. But that didn't mean her worshipful feelings had changed. At school, during midday lulls, Melanie liked to liven things up by going around the lunch table and making each girl disclose the identity of her crush, and the moment it was her turn Bree would pause, look down at her tray, try not to smile. "No one" would be her faltering response, a performance that was tedious for Mari to watch. She could only imagine how bad it had to be for Imogen.

Yet Imogen continued to invite them both—not actually invite, because inviting was a nicety no longer needed, but simply to accept that on any given weekend Bree and Mari would be coming over. By the eighth grade, they had reached an unspoken agreement that among the three houses, Imogen's was the one they preferred—the closest to school, the most comfortable, the coziest, her parents visibly amused by their enthusiasms. As if in anticipation, the pantry at Imogen's house was kept magically full. Every

Friday afternoon they would find it restocked with the snacks they liked most: cheese-flavored popcorn, kettle-cooked potato chips, the dark chocolate biscuits with the picture of the French schoolboy pressed into them. No oranges or bananas looking tired in a fruit bowl on the counter, but a basket of washed strawberries chilling in the refrigerator, or freshly cut cubes of pineapple, waiting to be eaten—which they wouldn't hesitate to help themselves to, feeling healthy in advance of phoning in their order at Dino's.

Imogen's father didn't complain about driving them to the video rental place, where the decision-making process was long and difficult, Mari going off on her own to comb through the old titles, in search of *A Taste of Honey* or *Billy Liar* or anything else about growing up working-class in the north of England, and Imogen and Bree tracking her down in the back of the store to say that the only black-and-white movie they would consent to was *Psycho*. Mari was in the thick of developing her sensibility, an essentially solitary endeavor, yet she liked doing so within earshot of familiar voices in the comedy section a few aisles away. Without a word she'd wander off, following the pulse of nameless feelings and associations, knowing that at some point her friends would have to come find her. When they did, they were bearing copies of *The Blues Brothers* and *Better Off Dead*, but in the end they settled on *Psycho*, not unhappily for Mari: Anthony Perkins had certain qualities—delicate features, button-down shirt, near-black hair, pained smile and perpetual unease—that marked him as probably belonging to the shadowbox she spent every spare moment assembling.

She was not alone in pursuing large, private, ongoing projects. It had become impossible to deny the fact that Bree's appearance was changing. The glasses were gone: her parents had finally relented and deemed her ready for soft contacts. Her hair, which she'd been growing out, turned red overnight—or Titian, as she described it jokingly, like Nancy Drew's. She corrected anyone who said she'd dyed it, pointing out that "henna is all-natural and actually good for you." Though she remained as short as Mari, she had grown confoundingly slim, and was now behaving like a thin person—wearing tops with spaghetti straps, slicing off the legs of her old jeans—and while Mari tried not to take it personally, she did experience an occasional pang of abandonment. *Cow* no longer applied in the affectionate plural.

Not all Bree's self-improvements were successful. One morning she arrived at school looking different in a way that Mari couldn't pinpoint.

"It's my eyebrows," Bree said. "You hold a pencil along the side of your nose and where the pencil meets your eyebrow, that's where you start plucking."

She took a yellow pencil from inside her desk and pressed it up to her cheek to demonstrate. Now Mari saw what was strange about Bree's face. She asked, "Are you supposed to pluck from that side of the pencil or *this* side?" and touched the raw gap between Bree's brows to show where she meant.

"Ohhhhhhhh." Bree exhaled, letting the pencil fall. "I wondered why mine didn't look like the picture. You're saying they're too far apart." She smiled bravely at Mari. "But that's what makeup is for, right? I can always fill them in."

The rigors of change did not discourage her. It required trial and error, dedication, regular servicing. She had taken to shaving not only her legs and armpits but also the tops of her feet, her underwear line, and rather weirdly, Mari thought, her forearms. She had figured out a way to isolate the body part she most despised—what she coldly called her double chin but was really just a little softness, a minor lack of definition—through a series of muscle contractions.

"It's like sucking in your stomach," she explained, "but instead I'm sucking in the area under my chin."

Mari confessed she hadn't noticed, and that in her opinion Bree's chin, her jawline, looked perfectly fine.

"That's because I'm sucking in *all the time*," Bree said. "I'm making it look fine."

Imogen usually didn't contribute to these conversations. There wasn't any disapproval in her silence, or squirminess, and she didn't act bored. It just felt as if she had politely stepped away for a moment. In fact, she seemed to have excused herself altogether from the fray—the consuming, frantic efforts of creating a self. She still looked like the girl who had befriended Mari in second grade, and Bree in sixth—same heavy curtain of hair, same orderly teeth and narrow body and marvelous skin—except that she was taller now, of course. She liked particular things but was not given to obsessions. She was known for being good at sports, singing in a clear contralto, and leading the student council with Cabinet-level skill. She was curious about other people. She could do complex math problems in her head. She had a delighted-sounding, unrestrained, bell-like laugh. When Mari stopped to think about it, her feeling of wonder was undimmed—what stroke of fortune had befallen her at age seven—for how did she ever get so lucky as to have Imogen as her friend?

But by the eighth grade there was something about Imogen that Mari couldn't quite put her finger on—that refused to be asked about, that was at once much bigger and subtler than the accident involving Bree's eyebrows— something that had to do with her sense of Imogen staging an imperceptible retreat. Imperceptible because she was still firmly at the center of everything: a school day felt desultory without her there, the weekend shapeless if not spent at her house. Yet Imogen occupied this position while also making herself absent. Sometimes literally—one Friday afternoon she startled Mari and Bree by appearing in her kitchen clad in the gym clothes she had brought home over the weekend to be washed. She passed right by them—they were standing in the pantry, opening a new box of Petit Écolier—and headed for the back door. "Where are you going?" they called after her. "Running," she called back. "On your own?" Mari asked incredulously. "For fun?" But Imogen didn't hear her; the door had already swung shut.

Still, she was Imogen; she commiserated and argued and teased; she planned birthday parties; she initiated cookie-eating contests; she filled the car or the locker room or the kitchen with her laugh; at the same time she was elsewhere, and Mari couldn't tell if her gaze was turned inward or directed at a spot so far in the distance that it was beyond Mari's ability to see.

For several months, Mari endured the uncertainty of whether she and her friends would be going to high school together. Life as she knew it felt suddenly provisional. Bree said that her family was waiting to see if the school would give them more financial aid, and then there was the question of where Bevin would be going, the possibility of added tuition. "Can't they just put her in public school until sixth grade," Mari asked, "like they did with you?" Imogen's having a sibling was also proving to be a problem, with her parents making her apply to the boarding school from which Nicholas was about to graduate, on the tiresome principle of exploring one's options. "But why be in someone else's shadow?" Mari said. As for Mari, she was threatening to enroll at her enormous local high school and take her chances on getting into the alternative program where students voted on things and called teachers by their first names—a threat that her mother failed to treat at all seriously.

In the end, Mari and Imogen and Bree decided to stay at their school. A relief that also felt slightly like a prison sentence. Four more years of all girls—and despite the promise of coed leadership conferences and community service outings, or the annual spring musical production with their so-called brother school, this felt like a long time.

The question of how and where to meet boys began to circulate among their classmates, gaining urgency, and resourcefully Bree started the summer by finding one in her backyard. Mari and Imogen were sitting cross-legged on the floor of Imogen's room, eating frozen fruit bars, when Bree told them. His name was Alex, he was fifteen, and he lived in the other half of her house.

"You don't understand," she said. "My parents aren't like yours. When I say they'll kill me, I'm not talking metaphorically. They *will* kill me."

"But all he said was hi," Mari clarified.

"And smiled," Bree said. "And then took his shirt off."

"That's something I always want to do," Imogen said, "when it's hot out and I'm playing basketball."

"The thing is," Bree said, "he hadn't even started playing yet."

Mari had been in Bree's backyard only a couple of times because it wasn't really a backyard, more like a paved-over area where extra cars could be parked. At one end a basketball net had been erected. Two wide wooden porches hung off the back of the house and overlooked the parked cars, or when there weren't any cars, a makeshift half-court. The porch on the first floor belonged to Bree's family, and it was where they kept the hibachi and Bevin's Big Wheel, along with her old stroller and play castle and other abandoned baby equipment.

"How did you not notice him before?" Mari asked.

"I did. He was just shorter then and a little chunky. There's four of them. My mom calls them the brood. You should hear them coming down the stairs in the morning." Bree wiped a drop of melted strawberry from the hairless expanse of her leg. "He's not the oldest but he's the tallest. Over the winter he got tall. And now he's practicing all the time out in the back. Not with the other kids—by himself."

Mari waited to see if Imogen wanted to say something. She herself was finding it hard to speak in the breathless tone that Bree seemed to expect of them. Finally she said, "I don't think there's anything for your parents to be worried about. That's normal, isn't it, for a neighbor to say hello. I say hello to our neighbors practically every day."

Bree smiled, almost sadly, as if at Mari's vast innocence. "This is different," she said. "Completely different."

"Because he took his shirt off?"

"No," Bree said, "because of the way he looked at me."

And how was that? (Mari didn't add *exactly* but wanted to.) Bree couldn't put it into words, she said. It was just a feeling. A back-and-forth. A spark. She frowned at the feebleness of her phrases. "This sounds arbitrary," she said, "but it's sort of like when you're about to take a test and you turn it over and read the first question and immediately you know the answer, and you know it's right? It's that feeling in your chest when you *know* you know it."

Mari felt her own chest growing tight as Bree spoke. She tossed her popsicle stick in the vicinity of the wastebasket and unexpectedly it went in. She tried summoning up the reason that Bree's family no longer spoke to their neighbors—was it the noise? Or something about a dog? A pitbull? Nor could she quite remember where they came from, though she was pretty sure it was somewhere that started with a *C*. They were either Cape Verdean, or Colombian. Or maybe Cambodian.

Bree was saying, "I could tell from the way he acted that he could feel *me* looking at him."

"He started missing the basket?" Imogen asked.

"Nothing that obvious. Though he did miss a few. It was more like he started walking and moving around in a different way, more slowly than before but also with more energy—"

Mari laughed abruptly. "You put a new spring in his step?"

"It was like he was slowly vibrating when he moved." Bree's voice was faraway, her face dignified. "And after he smiled at me, he never looked over at me. Not once. Not even when it would have been natural to glance in my direction. He made himself not look. And that's how I could tell."

"Well, just try not to get pregnant," Mari said flatly.

But Bree was too happy, exalted, to even roll her eyes at this remark.

Bree didn't get pregnant that summer, but she did end up having sex, and more than once. When Mari found out, her numb first thought was, But I was only kidding. The acceleration induced a sort of whiplash: How was it possible that Mari and Imogen, who between them had never kissed a single boy, or held hands with a boy, who didn't really know any boys, had a friend who was now experienced at having sex?

Bree told them nothing at the time. Throughout the summer, she offered up a handful of distracting details: notes written and exchanged, with the play castle as mailbox; late-night meetings by the trash cans, parents not registering a new readiness to take out the garbage. Brief conversations on the back-porch steps; spasms at the sound of a screen door swinging open. Mari imagined a forbidden love unfolding chastely in a Revere that was gritty and poorly lit but in a picturesque way, as if Bree had been cast in a community theater production of *West Side Story*.

The whole time, however, actual real-life sex was being had. And not with Alex, the vaguely brown boy next door, but with Nicholas. Nicholas Pickett. Imogen's brother was home for the summer before he went off to college, and Bree had sex with him. Or he had sex with Bree. Even years later Mari wasn't sure, when forming the sentence in her head, who to make the subject and who the object of the preposition.

Since you're not on FB I don't know if you saw but no small feat getting bus up and running. Jon very handy to be fair but I gravely underestimated. Bought it for a song then fell down down down down rabbit hole of repairs. Talk about a money pit!!! Remember when we saw that movie? At Circle Cinemas. Starring Shelley Long and I can't remember who played her husband. I think it scarred me. Seriously I have flashbacks whenever Jon starts looking at fixer uppers online believing himself secret real estate genius. Of course superior me I landed on biggest fixer upper of all. The moral is never buy school bus off Craigslist.

Imogen's house didn't have an ordinary backyard: what stretched behind her house was more like a woodland garden. Everything shady and dense, with only a small, irregular-shaped patch of lawn. A little creek ran through the greenery, and though you couldn't always see it, you could always hear the trickling sound it made. The creek was so narrow you could step over it easily, but nevertheless a low stone bridge had been built. Moss grew in abundance, also ferns and hostas. A mass of rhododendron turned different shades of pink in the spring. Knee-high statues rose up at random from the undergrowth: an upright frog with arms akimbo, two cherubs grappling, a rabbit absorbed in reading a book. In the sun-speckled depths of the garden stood an obelisk and several urns.

When they were much younger, Imogen and Mari played there after school. Back then there was less statuary and a little more wilderness, also a primitive tree house and a rope swing and a short zip line. Mari was afraid of heights, afraid of insects, wary of dirt, alert to poison oak, always dodging spiderwebs whether they were there or not. The only pants she owned had an elastic waist and were made of velour. Yet Imogen didn't despair of her. She remained cheerfully deaf to worries and complaints. Unflappably, she coached Mari over boulders and under fallen branches and through soggy patches. She didn't sigh when Mari lost her balance or needed to stop and catch her breath. Despite Mari's hopelessness, Imogen kept inviting her over to play, week after week—months passing, and then years.

Mari would not forget it: the feel of Imogen's bony grip on her wrist as she pulled her up through the rough opening in the tree-house floor.

The summer before high school began, the girls barely ventured out to the backyard. Maybe once or twice to hose off their feet, or to find mint to put into a pitcher of lemonade. Mari's second attempt at smoking occurred early one morning, alone, beneath the crabapple tree. Sometimes they would drape their bathing suits on the Adirondack chairs to make them dry faster, but usually they just hung them up in the bathroom. Bree always seemed to forget where she'd left her clothes and so had to run through the house in her damp bikini searching for them, squealing with cold.

Since it was summer and they were going into high school, they could sleep over not only on Fridays but on other days of the week as well. On one such night Mari stumbled upon Bree pushing open the French doors from the outside, stepping into the living room from the garden. She scared Mari nearly half to death. What on earth had she been doing out there? It was late—the middle of the night—Mari didn't know what time it was. She had awoken with a terrible thirst that only not-from-concentrate orange juice could quench and was making her silent way to the kitchen.

For a moment Bree didn't seem to see her. Her face was blank, and she was barefoot, wearing the oversized T-shirt she had put on before bed.

"You gave me a heart attack!" Mari whispered, and Bree jumped, sucked in her breath. "What are you doing up?" Mari asked, but before Bree could answer, a large shape appeared behind her in the doorway. It was Nicholas, dressed in his regular clothes, the same khaki shorts and wrinkled white Oxford he'd worn during the day. He wasn't wearing any shoes.

"Hi Nicholas," Mari said automatically. And then, stupidly: "I was just getting some orange juice. I think I might be coming down with something."

The words issued forth without her thinking. As if she were apologizing, as if she were the one who had interrupted or disturbed.

And this would be the moment when she knew. Without needing it spelled out for her, without questions and answers. She would take it all in—the late hour, the naked feet, the two bodies standing in the darkness, one right behind the other—and she would understand. She would see them, and she would know, and Bree would know that she knew. The two of them knowing it together.

Which wasn't how it happened, to be clear. This was solely the strange fantasy that Mari had concocted—her unwitting discovery, her reservoir of intuition. A look shared between her and Bree in the shadowy living room, followed by an understanding beyond her years.

So first it was engine that needed to be replaced. No big surprise there. Otherwise bus would still be in use right? But who knew diesel engines cost A LOT. Like down payment on a small house a lot. Then brakes failed inspection. FYI bus has air brakes not hydraulic brakes and air brakes are of course way more! Imogen literally saved our lives by paying for complete overhaul new compressor new lines new valves the WORKS. Plus labor. She wanted everything all new. Our third day a deer jumps out right in front of us and was I ever glad for brand new brake system! Whole process one miracle after another. Stunning moments of kindness from unforeseen sources. Largely reaffirmed my faith in humanity which was at low ebb for multiple reasons as I'm sure you can relate. It was Jon who after much arguing and defensiveness overcame my reluctance re fundraising page. He said people want to help and website just makes it easier to do so and though I hate to admit when he's right he was right.

Mari didn't stumble upon Nicholas and Bree in the middle of the night. And at no point that summer did Bree confide in her. She had to be told—by Melanie, of all people—while flipping through the new-imports bin at a record store near one of the unavoidable universities. They were music shopping before the start of school. Melanie didn't break down but seemed instead to expand under the weight of her conscience. Her eyes welled up as she told Mari, but Mari remained stony. It was only when her mother picked her up at the end of the afternoon that she slammed the passenger door shut and wept.

Her mother, who was a tentative driver to begin with, drove home extra slowly, as if steering a small craft through a squall. Mari had resolved not to say anything, but that resolve was hard to maintain once she was inside the warm hull of her mother's Toyota. She couldn't identify what hurt more: the fact that Bree had had sex; or that she had had sex with their best friend's brother; or that somehow with all her dumb vamping she'd actually won the attention of golden, unattainable Nicholas; or that she, Mari, had to hear about it secondhand from a random person like Melanie. It was like probing for the fracture in a limb that was entirely alight with pain. As she sobbed, her mother kept asking mundane questions: "Is Bree fifteen now?" (No, fourteen, her birthday isn't until the end of October), and "Does she still live in Revere?" (Yes, obviously), and "Remind me: How old is Nicholas?" (Eighteen! They had that big party with the tent, you were there). Questions with easy answers, the sort Coach Bell would ask when you banged heads with another girl while playing field hockey in PE class.

At home Mari's mother guided her in through the front door, made a pot of tea, and then parted and brushed her hair. Once she finished both braids, she said quietly, "You have to tell Imogen, and I have to tell her parents." She was standing behind Mari, who was seated in a kitchen chair. Mari didn't see why Imogen's parents needed to know anything, and said so, but her mother then began to undo and rebraid her hair as she explained the meanings of several legal terms: "age of consent"; "statutory rape"; "liability." When she stepped from behind Mari's chair to turn on the faucet, Mari saw the look on her face. She feared for an awful moment that her mother was about to cry. But she didn't; she rinsed out the teacups and scrubbed the pans left soaking in the sink and paused only to look up briefly and say in midthought, to either Mari or her own reflection in the window, "They opened their home to her."

Imogen looked so plainly delighted when asked to return to the tree house that Mari felt like a monster. "We haven't been up here in ages," Imogen said, and stretched her arms up, oblivious to the accumulation of cobwebs. "Look! I'm hitting the ceiling now."

But as Mari talked, Imogen's arms sank back down to her sides. She bent over so she could rest her elbows on the filthy edge of the window, and she allowed her sheet of hair to fall forward and hide her face. Mari knew that she was crying, but she also knew not to put her arm around her smotheringly. When Imogen finally spoke, she didn't turn to look at her. "This whole time I thought Alex was the one she liked."

Her voice had a hitch in it, and that made Mari start to cry.

"I thought so too. I mean, that's what she told us. But maybe she was just using him as a cover? I don't know if there was anything really there."

Imogen was silent for a moment.

"Maybe she wanted to talk about what she was feeling without having to say who the person was."

Mari nodded tearfully. "Right. Like a decoy."

Imogen continued to stare out the window.

Another possible explanation suddenly reared up in Mari's mind, and she felt her stomach lurch. Maybe Alex had been not decoy but *practice*. Like a warm-up. Low stakes, no pressure. Vaguely brown, formerly chubby Alex. Like shooting baskets in the backyard before the game. She shuddered. She could never say that aloud.

"You know what," Imogen said, "I really wish they hadn't taken down the zip line."

Mari joined her in gazing at the yard. Below them spread a low layer of broad, glossy foliage. It looked like a shimmering green carpet that floated just a few inches above the ground, lush but uncomfortable to lie down in. In, not on, because of course the carpet wasn't solid but made out of large, stiff-leaved plants that would crowd in on you or get crushed under you if you were to try to have sex in their midst. This was part of the strangeness of Mari's fantasy—there really was no welcoming spot in this woodland garden for two people looking to have sex. Or at least sex according to how she imagined it. To her mind it required a reasonably comfortable surface, one that was by necessity horizontal. Never in a million years would she consider the following possible: on the hood of a Volvo; folded over a table; standing on one foot, pushed up soundlessly against a bathroom door.

How did they begin the conversation with Bree?

We need to talk to you. About something serious.

Or: *Melanie told us.*

Or: *Will you close the door?*

Or: *I don't even know what to say right now.*

All plausible, but none certain. None sounding even faintly familiar. However hard she tried, Mari couldn't remember. Not what was said, or where. The total blankness made her wonder if a conversation had ever happened. Did Imogen speak alone with Bree? Was Mari not a party to it? Did parents step in and make arrangements among themselves, with the thought of sparing them the pain of talking? Or was Mari's mere presence during this conversation ignoble enough that her memory now refused to summon it? All plausible, too.

What Mari did know was that whatever happened in such a conversation, however the information was conveyed, Bree would remember. She would be able to recall every detail of it clearly.

Just as Mari could recall where she and Melanie had been standing in the record store that August afternoon;

what Melanie was wearing (a saggy blue cardigan over her Buzzcocks shirt); what they had just eaten (roll-up sandwiches with tahini dressing); what was playing on the store's speakers (Nick Cave doing a cover of "Hey Joe").

Another detail, impossible to forget: the phrase that Nicholas had pressed into her, hotly and permanently, a phrase describing her mother. During one of the phone calls between her mother and Imogen's, Nicholas had picked up the receiver in another part of the house—an interruption that wouldn't even be possible now—and spoken at her mother furiously, in the relentless, punishing style of a seasoned debater. Afterward she'd walked into Mari's room looking dazed. "He called me, among many other unpleasant things," her mother had said, sinking onto the bed, "a busybody. A pathetic busybody who wants to make everyone else as miserable as I am."

A cooling of relations ensued, but despite what Bree later claimed, it couldn't be rightly called a banishment. The interlude resembled more of a breather, a period of recovery, than an actual estrangement. After their talk in the tree house, Mari had pictured Imogen and herself moving side by side down the school hallways, heads bowed like novitiates, with Bree maintaining a respectful distance, back turned to them as she spun and spun the combination dial on her locker. And for the first weeks of high school they

did give her some space. But not unkindly. They continued to exchange smiles with her; they offered to loan her a
pen when she needed one; they waved and said hello, liked
her new jacket, laughed when she said something funny in
class, held the door open for her.

Being a duo again brought with it the ease of traveling light. Maybe Mari's mother hadn't been completely
wrong about two being less complicated. On some days it
felt good, the way depriving yourself during Lent felt good,
the invigoration of being disciplined and lean. But on some
days it was terrible not having Bree at her side, and Mari
walked through the school building feeling wobbly and exposed, buffeted by air, as if riding along bumpily in a jeep
without a door. In the lunchroom she watched from the
corner of her eye as Bree made forays into other groups—
for a while she joined the musically gifted girls, the ones
who spent their Saturdays at the conservatory, and then she
seemed to hit it off with a new girl named Pam who lived
in a town even farther away than Revere. There were also
the two Allisons, whom she'd always liked and been chatty
with. She never sat by herself, in other words; she wasn't
friendless.

One day Mari saw her leave the lunchroom holding the
palm tree–covered cosmetics bag in which she carried her
tampons, and briefly felt sick with missing her.

But in only a few months, they were back to being
friends. The three of them had been placed in the same
advanced French class, with sublimely silly M. Bernard,
and it was hard not to sit together when there was so much

goofiness and group work and all the ridiculous skits going on. Then, separately, Imogen and Bree became possessed by the crazy idea of rowing crew, Bree as a coxswain and Imogen as a bow, and before long they were all at Imogen's house on a Friday night, eating Dino's. Lifting a slice of Hawaiian pizza from the box, Bree asked, "Am I off probation now?" and even though she asked it sincerely, without any sarcasm or humor, Mari and Imogen both laughed gently, as if she'd made a sweet but impenetrable joke. And so they picked up again, the three of them. The various parents supported it, some more cautiously than others, on the understanding that certain ground rules would be observed.

If Mari was being honest, however, she would admit that even as their friendship continued—and it did continue, ever-shifting in closeness and distance, through high school and college and deep into adulthood—she carried with her an unwanted residue, a sort of fine, nearly invisible grit she'd tracked in without noticing. Hard little traces of something that refused to be swept or smoothed away. When Mari eventually brought a boy around—it took a while—she had to brace herself. She was watchful. Noting the moments Bree turned her smile on him, or touched his arm, or looked up at him from under her tumble of hennaed hair. And all her tireless self-grooming—it was no longer a curiosity but a threat. The absurd amount of time Bree needed to prepare herself before leaving the house— enraging, resentment-stirring. Mari knew it was unfair to feel this way. Unfair to perceive what would have been merely annoyances in another friend as evidence in Bree of a failing that had already revealed itself, treacherously. But this was how she felt. She couldn't help it.

Are your parents still living at same address? That question was original impetus for now epic length text! So saddened by news of Imogen's parents selling theirs. Hard to think of them in a condo. I hope yours have stayed put for now—can't imagine all those paintings and plants belonging anywhere else. My first time at your house I thought I was inside museum! But seriously I loved stillness and calm and smell of soil from all the pots. I can't walk past a bromeliad without thinking of your mom.

I'm ashamed it's taken me this long to send proper thank you note. Also the kids tanks. Hahaha tanka. Sent email of gratitude immediately via website but want to do something better for her. Every time I pull food from fridge or turn on stove or put clothes in washer I thank her. All our tiny appliances. As lifesaving as the brakes! Please send her my love and confirm address. Also update from you please! No need to write 19 c. Novel like this one but miss you and want to hear how you are. xoxoxoxo

Mari felt unsteady. She had to put down her phone. She felt a shrinking all over her body, and then a wave of prickling, an intolerable heat.

How had she not told Bree about her mother?

She didn't need to calculate how long it had been. She

knew it already; she knew it down to the day. On Saturday it would be four months. Four months, plus the preceding six months of treatment, and in all that time she hadn't managed to tell her.

There had been long spells of silence before, on both sides—growing longer as they themselves grew older. Mari hadn't known, for instance, about the beetle study, or the bus. She couldn't remember if she'd mentioned to Bree anything about their moving. She sent holiday cards every year; they texted each other on their birthdays with strings of fond, exuberant emojis. There was no sense of neglect, no recriminations, between the two of them, or none as far as she knew. But this omission on Mari's part was different— not in degree but in kind. It was a disgrace.

Her mother had made a donation, clearly, and by the sound of it not a small one. This was Mari's first time hearing of it. Which was surprising, considering that throughout her treatment her mother had been nearly obsessed by the task of getting her accounts in order and taking care of what she called housekeeping. She had enlisted Mari in cataloging the paintings, for instance. She'd said that Mari's father wouldn't remember where they had come from, which ones were valuable and which not. She was also preoccupied by the kind of food he was feeding the cats. Mari kept bringing her back to more important matters—financial paperwork, friends she wanted to see. Yet her mother hadn't said anything about Mari's friend, or the fundraising page, or the money she'd given her.

Mari wondered if her gift might have had something

to do with the news—her mother used to refer to herself somewhat indulgently as a cable news junkie, someone who canceled plans in order to stay home and watch Senate hearings or follow fast-breaking stories—and so much of the recent news had made that particular summer feel close again. The past looked different now, and especially the sex. It was likely they had seen it all wrong back then. Why was Bree the bad apple? The one needing to be banished? How could a girl of fourteen be the one held responsible? This wasn't the first time such questions had occurred to Mari: she was a feminist, for heaven's sake; she did go to college. But maybe all the zeitgeisty talk had led Mari's mother to reconsider what had happened decades earlier, and if it wasn't too strong a word, to repent of her part in it.

The thought was desolating. Her mother—her practical, refined, brisk, unsentimental, highly opinionated and discerning mother—was capable of experiencing a change of heart, when Mari was not. For all the years she had spent fancying herself a sensitive person, cultivating her feelings and perceptions, her heart had remained tough. Unyielding. No matter how hard she tried to view the past from an enlightened perspective, no matter how much she wanted to see it with clearer eyes, her heart kept stubbornly placing Bree as the subject of the sentence. As agent and initiator. The active, desiring, incautious subject. That was her friend, the girl she remembered. But her mother, evidently, had come to see things differently.

———

LIKES

Bree was the one who invented the names. They evolved over time, as nicknames tend to do. First came Imogen's—it wasn't so far to get from Pickett to Pickle. This was probably in the seventh grade. The name suited her precisely because it was so perfectly wrong. Nothing salty or squat about Imogen, the very last person you'd expect to find inside a dark, briny barrel—which was why it must have been so satisfying to call her that. After months of being addressed almost exclusively as Pickle—your turn, Pickle; can you pass me that, Pickle; merci beaucoup, Pickle—Imogen answered one day with, "You're welcome, Brickle"—for obvious reasons. And so Bree became Brickle, a name that eventually got shortened to Brick. Upon the introduction of Brickle, Bree made the regal decision that Mari had to have a name, too. During lunch she led them into the school library and heaved open the giant dictionary resting on its stand. She flipped through chunks, then leafed through single pages, then stopped and peered down at an entry.

"Good news!" Bree said. "Guess what it means." Her finger inched across the page. "*Mickle* means 'much, or a large amount' as in the phrase 'Many a little makes a mickle.' And guess where it means that?"

Behind her glasses, her face was lit up.

"Guess."

Imogen and Mari couldn't guess.

"In Northern England." She smiled at them exultantly. "Where Manchester is!" she crowed, as if Mari's happiness was her own.

THE BURGLAR

He watches the second car back out of the driveway and then he makes a slow lap around the block, careful not to step on the cracks in the sidewalk. From other houses come the sounds of dogs barking, and from other yards the noise of lawn mowers and leaf blowers. Construction is happening somewhere down the street. After completing the lap he looks up at the clock on top of the Catholic church the next block over: 9:40. He walks up the driveway purposefully and pushes through the white wooden gate, a high gate that, he noticed yesterday, doesn't have a lock.

. . .

Ecola? Orkin? Idling at the intersection she can't remember for a moment the name of the company she is on her way home to meet. In the past week three men came through the house, one after the other, wearing jumpsuits and slipping disposable booties over their shoes, three men on their hands and knees in the attic, creaking overhead, tapping inquisitively at the beams. After collecting all the estimates, she consulted with her husband, who had only this to say: "Trust your gut." Oh—Greenleaf! That's the name. They cost the most, but she liked the man and, according to the literature, they use 100-percent-organic materials.

. . .

The husband is late to work. As the elevator carries him up to the offices, he is thinking about Emmett Byron Diggs, Attica inmate #17864. Diggs will be the first innocent man to appear on the show. When the showrunner put him on the episode, he said, "I don't want you to think that I'm asking you to write this one just because the character is black," and he replied, "I don't think that." But now he is beginning to worry about what to do with Emmett Diggs.

. . .

Two thousand one hundred seventy-five dollars: This she remembers exactly. After the job is done, she will write out the entire amount and the feel of the check tearing crisply along the perforated line will be a small, silly thing that pleases her. Thank you so much! For the first time since moving into the house, she is not worrying every minute about money. She is going to the gym again. She is washing her car on a regular basis. In her clean car, in her damp gym clothes, she drives through the bright blue morning, feeling calm. She's going to be right on time.

. . .

He tips back in his chair and looks at the whiteboard, where the story beats for Act One have been written in streaky black marker. They're only two days in to breaking the Emmett Diggs episode. So far the formula has been consistent: 1960s bad guy commits heinous crimes, winds up in solitary at Attica, travels through a rift in the space-time continuum, and pops up in present-day upstate New York, where he continues his crime spree until he is tracked down and apprehended by a top-secret team of special agents. Which the network says they like; which has worked just fine until now; so why, on the first episode he's been assigned to write, are they trying something different?

. . .

The backyard is a mess. Weeds up to his waist, cracked concrete. A tarp slung over a pile of stuff pushed up against the garage door. From the front, the house looked nice. Neat. Green lawn. Front door painted a glossy bright red. But back here it's different. Flattened cardboard boxes, dusty grill. Plastic playhouse bleaching in the sun. Shrunken lumps of shit all over the dead grass. He hesitates, then thinks of the cars that pulled out of the driveway: a Prius, a Mini Cooper. There will definitely be Apple gear inside.

. . .

Episode 103, "Frankie Sutton": a deadly bank robber returns from the past to take a half dozen hostages at gunpoint during a holdup of the First Niagara Bank. Episode 104, "Walter Buckley": the notorious "Loose Cannon" bomber plants a pipe bomb in the Buffalo Field Office of the FBI. Episode 107, "Mark David Dixon": a serial child murderer kidnaps Special Agent O'Hare's nephew from a local playground and leaves the team a trail of taunting clues. And now Episode 110, "Emmett Diggs": an innocent black man convicted for the grisly murder of his white fiancée emerges out of the ether and does what, exactly?

. . .

At the stop sign, she counts to five. She doesn't want to get another ticket. And then waits a little more, because there's Jessica, her neighbor, out walking Buster. She gives a tap on her horn and waves: Go ahead, cross the street. She isn't in any hurry, and she's preoccupied with a relaxing and anticipatory sort of arithmetic. How many more weeks before they can talk about getting some bids on the roof? Also, the kid needs a proper bookcase; the shelves in her room are starting to bow. The Voder-Smith family is ready to graduate from Swedish-designed particleboard! They'll have to plan ahead for property taxes, due at the beginning of December, but if all goes as it should they won't have to ask her mother for help this year. And if—is even to think it to jinx it? Her husband is superstitious about these things—*if* the show gets an order for nine more episodes, maybe they can finally tackle the backyard.

. . .

On one side of the board, possible backstories for Emmett Diggs: 1. Arthritic gardener's son, recently home from the army; 2. Head chef in the kitchen of local country club; 3. Member of the maintenance staff at Miss So-and-So's School. Behind each of these possibilities is the question: How does a black man in 1961 gain entry to the spaces where rich white girls live, so that he can fall in love with one, get secretly engaged, and then be accused of murder when she is found dead, raped and mutilated, on a golf course? Another question, asked only by the husband, and only in his head: How does a science-fiction guy end up writing racial melodrama? Also: How do I write this character without making him seem like all the other decent, long-suffering, wrongly accused black men who have shown up onscreen over the years?

. . .

Spit. Spraying across the glass. The barking sudden and loud. A black dog at the back door, lunging at him from the other side of the window in the door. It looks big, maybe seventy-five pounds. It looks from its light eyebrows as if it might have some Rottweiler mixed in. The door shakes when the dog launches itself, its nails scrabbling on the glass. Through the window, beyond the dog, he can see the washer and dryer, he can see sweatshirts and jackets hanging from hooks, cleaning supplies lined up along a shelf. Not too far from the back door to the shelf, the distance no more than the length of his arm, outstretched. And the dog, now that he's had a minute to look at it? Not as big as its bark makes it sound.

. . .

We open on a couple, embracing in the dark. The grounds of a golf course roll away on all sides, the grass metallic in the moonlight. From nearby, the ticking of sprinklers and, farther off, mingled voices and the clink of silverware and glass, the warm commotion of a party. We push in on their faces, mouths locked, her skin almost ghostly against the darkness of his, his fingers black stripes moving through the pale waves of her hair. The kissing deepens, their bodies pressed close, she reaching up to slip from her shoulder the fragile strap of her dress, but with a single touch he stops her, his large hand over hers. Still kissing her, he cups her head lightly in his hands. Her eyes close; his open. A strangely empty gaze. In an instant his grip tightens, his arms contracting, a sudden twist. The sickening crack of bone. He's broken her fucking neck! Off his glazed look we cut to titles. "Could that work?" Lenny, the story editor, glances hopefully from the showrunner to the husband to the other writers sitting loose-limbed around the table. "For the teaser?"

. . .

Only two blocks away from home, she feels her sense of well-being begin to sour around the edges. She's using half a personal day for this. And that's not including the hours she spent online, clicking back and forth between company websites and sifting through contradictory user reviews, followed by even more hours imprisoned in the house, waiting for the men to show up with their slip-on booties and clipboards and brochures. In her heart, she sees Slash, guitarist for Guns N' Roses, his pet boa constrictor draped across his bare shoulders, staring morosely at a puddle spreading at the foot of his Sub-Zero refrigerator. Years and years before, when asked by an interviewer how his life had changed since the success of *Appetite for Destruction*: "I got this house and my refrigerator is leaking all over the place and I feel comfortable just leaving it that way, but I can't do that, 'cause this is my house."

· · ·

The shock of the door flying open makes the dog skitter backward, but soon enough it's on him, snarling, his shirt in its teeth, its weight pulling him down, but look who's got hold of the Windex. So there. For a streak-free shine. Right in the eyes, buddy. Who's scary now?

· · ·

What sort of crimes are committed by an unjustly incarcerated man who's traveled through a rift in the space-time continuum? There's not much for our team of special agents to do if Attica inmate #17864 pops up in present-day New York and spends his days being decent. Hence the episode's twist: Emmett Diggs is now a cold-blooded killer. Hunting down women who resemble his dead fiancée and ritualistically murdering them in exactly the same way that she was killed on the golf course. The husband locks his gaze on the water bottle sitting in front of him so that his eyes don't start rolling involuntarily. Emmett Diggs: a saint *and* a predator. The husband can't look at Lenny right now, can't look at the whiteboard; he feels his insides slowly curdling. He's not going to win any NAACP Image Awards for this script, that's for sure. His first episode of network television, and he doesn't want his mom and dad to watch it.

· · ·

Oh, but there it is: her house. Home. Eaten out of house and home. But not quite yet—help is on the way. The termites chittering in their tiny villain voices: *Foiled again!* An upwelling of love as she turns in to the driveway and sees the white gate and the red door. It's the prettiest bungalow on the block. The Craftsman clapboard container of their lives. Overpriced, yes; heavily mortgaged and termite-infested, yes; but it's theirs. The feeling of four walls and a roof over your head, of turning a big cardboard box upside down and cutting out a hole for a window, drawing a door in magic marker, taking up residence inside. *Safe!* the umpire cries. There's no van parked at the curb, no sign of Greenleaf; she's beaten them home.

· · ·

Finger on the trigger of the spray bottle, he backs the dog through the kitchen, then the living room, across a short hallway, and into the bathroom. Not ideal, as he'd like to take a look at what's inside the medicine cabinet, but it's the only room he's encountered so far where he can close the door. Or maybe not. The latch won't hold. The door pops ajar as soon as he pushes it shut. Which he does, without success, several times in a row. And now the dog is barking again, insanely. He tries once more, not slamming it but just pressing it firmly in that careful way you have to handle old things. He pauses, counts to three, slowly draws his hand away. The door springs open. Ridiculous. Now he's going to have to maneuver the dog out of the bathroom and into the half-furnished guest room, down the hall. His Windex is ready. But seriously: a bathroom with a door that doesn't close? How do people live like that?

. . .

We open on a man sauntering down a quiet block, hands in pockets, whistling "Smoke Gets in Your Eyes." Just daring someone, anyone, to stop him. Can't a man enjoy a stroll through a pleasant neighborhood in the middle of the day? He pulls his large hands from the pockets of his checkered chef's pants and wishes he'd had a chance to change into something sharp. The houses gaze back at him, cool and inviting. Maybe not quite as grand as you'd expect, only two blocks away from the country club. But still nice. Still desirable. He looks at the windows and imagines who's living inside. Who might be brushing her hair over the sink, or writing in her diary. Doing stomach-flattening exercises in her underwear. Leafing through a catalog, fiddling with the radio, rinsing out a juice glass, all the while a man is walking by and looking at her windows. Why shouldn't he look: It's the goddamn twenty-first century. There's a brother in the White House. Any one of these places, Emmett thinks, could be mine.

. . .

As soon as she walks through the front door she hears his footsteps overhead. "Doug? You're still home?" She wonders what could possibly make him run so late. Because won't that be noted? If he just moseys into the room after all the other writers are there? Her husband, working so hard to get this job. The multiple spec scripts, the rounds of fruitless general meetings. Finally to get a break—based solely on his writing sample! And now he's going to be the guy who shows up late.

. . .

With the dog yelping in the guest room, he takes the stairs two at a time. "Always start with the master" is his motto. But what a corny word, *motto*, never to be used again, not even in his head. And it turns out to be not much of a master: the ceiling sloped, the bed unmade, the pillows strewn sloppily about. He peels a pillow out of its sham—fuck! how does he even know that's what it's called?—and uses the empty case to catch the stuff he's scooping from a jewelry box divided into a crazy-making number of small compartments. Good stuff? Bad stuff? He'll sort it out later. Digging through the dresser drawers yields nothing. Where do they keep the watches? He circles the room pointlessly, and the floor vibrates slightly beneath him as the front door slams shut. "Doug?" a woman's voice calls from below. "You're still home?" He drops the sham.

. . .

Her husband doesn't answer. She goes to the bottom of the stairs and calls his name again. Is he on the phone? It could be work-related, in which case she shouldn't keep hollering in the background. She hears more footsteps and a man's voice from the bedroom: "It's just us. Just the cleaning crew."

. . .

Cleaning crew? Where did that come from? More like a break-in crew. Break-in crew? Ha! Breakin' crew! He cracks himself up sometimes, he really does. His whole body is shaking. *Breakin' 2, Electric Boogaloo. Breakin' 2, Electric Boogaloo.* He's going to have that shit bouncing around in his head all day.

. . .

"Oh! Hi!" She is briefly confused. "Did my husband let you in?" He must have made it to work on time. "Please let me know if you need anything, okay?" she calls up the stairs. "Or if you want something to drink?" There's still soda left in the refrigerator from when her in-laws visited. How funny to say *cleaning crew*—but then again who would want to call themselves *exterminators*? The phone starts ringing in the kitchen: either her mother or the dentist's office or the Music Center looking for a donation. Nobody else calls on the landline anymore.

. . .

From below, a robotic murmur: *Beep-beep-beep-beep-beep.* Pause. *Beep-beep-beep-beep-beep.* Fuck! Forget the master.

Forget the pillow sham. Grab the laptops and go. The office is down the hall from the bedroom. Keep it simple. In and out of the office, down the stairs, through the front door, and you're gone.

. . .

"Hello?" She picks up the handset, dropping her keys and gym bag on the counter, and notices for the first time that Misha isn't in his crate. Did Doug put him in the back-yard? She's told him how many times that the dog's pee-ing on her tomato plants—the only things worth saving out there—and can't be left unsupervised. The woman on the other end of the line is saying that her name is Gloria. She's asking, "Is this Maggie Voder, at 541 North Arden Boulevard?"

. . .

There's Spawn, Spider-Man, Neo and Morpheus, the Crow. A really nice selection, but they've been taken out of their boxes, which is retarded, and arranged on a shelf above the computer and the desk. At least the comic books are stored properly: long white cardboard boxes line the walls, and he knows that if he lifts a lid he will find the books inside bagged and boarded, organized by artist or series or year. He would like to sit on the floor for a while and see what's in there, fingering through the issues, granting or withholding his approval, losing track of time. How often has he opened one of his own boxes, just to check on some small detail, the first appearance of a minor character, only to look up a moment later and discover that the day has disappeared?

. . .

"Yes, this is Maggie," she says into the phone. She has it tucked under her ear and is wandering back to the foot of the stairs so that she can adjust the thermostat. She's still sticky from the gym and wants to turn on the air. Gloria explains that she is calling from Greenleaf. That she's very sorry for the inconvenience but she's just spoken to the technician who's got stuck in traffic on the 101 and should be arriving at 541 North Arden Boulevard no later than— "He's already here," she tells Gloria, just as she sees him for the first time, coming down the staircase. She smiles at him. He's African American! Good for Greenleaf.

. . .

The front door now seems impossibly far away: There's a woman standing at the bottom of the staircase and beaming up at him. For a moment, he can't figure out who she is. She's short, squat, sweaty, brownish, her ponytailed hair frizzing around her face. The nanny? So where's the woman who called up to him—the lady with the voice? As he inches farther down the stairs, he catches himself saying again, idiotically, "Just the cleaning crew," like it's the magic password that will get him safely out the door.

. . .

Who does he remind her of? Oh right—that kid from the Disney Channel who's now competing on *Dancing with the Stars.* The eyes wide set, the face a little too broad, the cheeks chubby, the smile ingratiating. That'll be something to tell Violet when she gets home from school. She always likes it when her mother pays attention to the Disney Channel universe. *You'll never guess*, she'll say, *who he looked exactly like . . .*

. . .

Emmett pauses in front of a house that reminds him, finally, of hers. Something about the sloping lawn and the red front door, or maybe it's just the tinging of the wind chimes and the way the midmorning light makes the house look picture-book flat. He strides up the driveway. He smooths his hair. Without hesitating, he walks across the grass and goes straight to the windows farthest on the right—where the sewing room would be—but instead of the little lace-covered table and the pedestaled fern he sees only a mattress and box spring, a set of barbells, a bicycle, and an enormous black dog, which has risen up on its hind legs, placed its front paws on the windowsill, and is barking at him miserably.

. . .

All in the same moment she hears, from behind the guest room door, Misha barking (Why did Doug put him in *there?*), and notices, on the man above her on the stairs, the absence of a Greenleaf uniform (freelancer?), and sees, draped across his body, a black messenger bag with the name and jazzy logo of her new employer (Hey, what a coincidence) . . .

. . .

"Just leaving now," he says, inching down the stairs.

. . .

She has the exact same messenger bag—given to her only a month ago by human resources on the day of her New Hire Orientation, and containing a huge three-ring binder holding the *Employee Conduct Handbook* as well as a reusable water bottle imprinted, like the bag, with her employer's logo. A bag that's remained untouched, she must confess, since she dumped it in a corner of their home office upon returning from the rather discouraging orientation. A bag that she hasn't bothered to empty but that, she sees now, is perfectly useful.

. . .

He can hear a tinny voice coming from the telephone. "Are you still there?" the voice asks, as the nanny shifts the receiver from one shoulder to the other. "Hello?"

. . .

"That's my bag." The sentence comes out of her mouth before she even knows what she is saying. "That's my bag," she says again, as he squeezes past her and makes for the front door. The dog is barking. The phone is in her hand. "Where are you going?" she hears herself asking. With the other hand, she reaches out and takes hold of the strap. Everything feels both fast and slow.

. . .

He's surprised by the way she asks it—"Where are you going?"—like it's a real question. Not like, *Where do you think you're going.* And not like, *You better not be going anywhere with that bag.* She asks as if she wasn't expecting him to leave, and can't imagine where in the world he could possibly be off to.

. . .

Let's see: Her husband's old laptop, which Violet uses to watch movies when they fly. The external hard drive that she bought last month but still hasn't taken out of the box. Her husband's off-brand noise-reducing headphones that she's been planning to replace at Christmas with a fancy pair, the real deal. All of it known to her and protruding from the messenger bag.

. . .

Trying to pull away from her, he says it once more: "Just leaving now!" But she's got a good firm grip on the bag, this lady, this nanny who's turned out to be the lady. She's grabbed hold of the bag, and somehow the weight of her hand on the strap has made it surprisingly heavy. "Ma'am, can you hear me?" comes faintly from the receiver. She ignores the voice and keeps looking at the bag. She doesn't look at him, just at the bag, or maybe she's looking at him as if he's an extension of the bag or the bag is an extension of him and she is claiming both. She won't let go. All he wants to do is get out the door and up the street and around the corner and back to his cousin's place but this sweaty woman gripping the strap won't let him.

. . .

The husband isn't hungry but it's time now to think about lunch. The menu from the Mediterranean place is circulating around the table, along with the sign-up sheet to write down orders. He doesn't think he can do the chicken panini again—it would be the third time this month, and the pesto aioli doesn't taste as good as it used to. No more fries on the side, either; he's starting to feel like shit. At first what had seemed like unbelievable bounty—the kitchen's always stocked with Pop-Tarts *and* Mexican Coke? The show buys us lunch *every day?*—now gives him a constant, low-grade stomachache. And, fuck it, who cares if eating kale is clichéd. He writes down a salad, and Lenny, at his elbow, lets out a little sigh of admiration. Lenny, plump as a partridge, who has asked on several occasions about his gym routine. "You eat smart," Lenny murmurs. "You work out smart. You're in the peak physical shape that a person can achieve." He shakes his head in wonderment as the husband hands off the menu, laughing.

. . .

With the dog still barking, Emmett rounds the corner of the house and ambles along its shady side, now and then glancing into a window. What is he looking for? He's suddenly not sure. The strange sense of purpose that brought him up the driveway and across the lawn has just as mysteriously deserted him. He drifts from window to window, and a part of him understands dimly that this is not the house he is looking for, that none of them are, that the house he is looking for and the girl who lives inside it are in some profound way no longer available to him. But he persists in his orbit of the house, for lack of any other direction. He reaches up to brush a bit of spiderweb from his face—the hedges are full of them—and when he does so is startled momentarily by the warmth of his own hand.

. . .

Automatically, she does the math. This has become an involuntary habit. When she got that ticket at the intersection, for instance—an outrageous amount, a stomach-twisting sum—she had paid it off by the time she reached home. By adding together the early-bird discount on Violet's school uniforms and the first-three-months-free promotion on their cable package and the unblemished hundred-dollar bill that her great-aunt still sends her every year on her birthday, she'd made the ticket disappear. Ta-da! And now, hanging on for dear life to the strap of her messenger bag, she takes one look at the belongings shoved inside and immediately assesses the damage as minimal: two hundred and fifty bucks, tops. She can make that go away, no problem.

. . .

"Okay," Lenny says, squinting at the board. "Okay, okay, okay." When he pitches, he can say up to a dozen *okays* in a row without even noticing before he gets his first real word out. "Okay, so we start with a dead girl on the golf course, right? And the next morning, our guys, when they see the way her body is arranged"—he quickly contorts himself to illustrate—"they know this has gotta be one of theirs. The cervical fracture, the pattern of lacerations, it all matches the profile. But they're confused, right? Because they have the benefit of hindsight. They know that the only thing Emmett Diggs was guilty of was being a black man who dared to love a white woman in 1961." He takes a gulp of air. "So what they can't figure out is: Who butchered the blonde lying next to the eighth hole? They spend the first two acts chasing down bad leads while Diggs stalks and seduces and kills one beautiful young victim after another—" The husband interrupts: "Lenny." He tries to find the easy tone he uses when giving the kid workout advice. "This direction we're going in—"

. . .

From inside the house, he thinks he hears movement, voices. A conversation. There's someone in there besides the barking dog, and the thought obscurely comforts him. He isn't alone, after all. He has somewhere to go now, someone to find. But he cannot summon up his whistling bravado from before; he is still hesitant and uneasy, and as he edges his way closer to the back steps he wishes he had a better idea of what he is supposed to do.

. . .

"It doesn't make sense to me. If you were Emmett Diggs and you'd been rotting away in Attica, wrongly convicted for murdering the love of your life, tormented by the prison guards, and then after being thrown into solitary yet again for something you didn't do, you suddenly find yourself free and at large and fifty years into the future—your first impulse is to go pick up women at the nearest country club?" That sounds more sarcastic than he wants it to. He needs to go slow. "I mean, wouldn't Diggs want to exonerate himself? He'd want justice." But who is he kidding; that's not the kind of show he's writing on. "Actually, vengeance. He wants to avenge her death. He's hunting down the real killer, whoever it was who murdered his fiancée and framed him for it." Lenny is nodding rapidly as if completely convinced but then asks politely, "Maybe that's a more familiar take on it?" The co-executive producer agrees: "I feel like I've already seen that a million times." The showrunner gives him an encouraging smile. "We're trying to do something different here," he explains. "Our mandate is to be edgy, to push the envelope."

. . .

She doesn't want to let go of the bag. Despite knowing what the contents are, and of how little value, despite being aware that there's nothing inside the bag that she wants or needs or even really likes, she won't let go. A treacherous thought occurs to her, unbidden: her husband must in some way be at fault. It all makes sense. He forgot to lock the door when he left for work that morning, which is why some guy, some stranger, was able to waltz into their house and have a look around and help himself to a bagful of their stuff. And now, like everything else concerning the house, she's going to have to take care of it. How dare he! Just one more pushy person trying to take advantage of her: the contractors with their ridiculous bids, the Korean dad in the Lexus who has twice cut her off in the carpool lane at school. Don't even get her started on Anne-Marie, the simpering but secretly ruthless head of HR, who managed to chisel away at her salary requirements until she was left with a comprehensive vision plan and three weeks' vacation while basically working for free. Well, enough is enough. They're not going to get away with it. She's sick and she's tired and she's not going to take it anymore. Where has she heard that before? Somehow nothing in this moment feels entirely her own, from the words in her head to the sneakers braced on the floor to the hand that is holding so tightly to the bag strapped across the man's body.

. . .

He's running out of time. He's only a few feet away from the front door. "Let go," he tells her, in a voice he doesn't quite recognize. Hopefully it sounds deep. And forceful? He's not even sure she's heard him. Her grip is still strong but her face has gone sort of blank.

. . .

The husband focuses on his breath, takes a second to re-group. He smiles back at the showrunner. "Okay," he says, "okay"—he's starting to sound like Lenny, for God's sake—"I guess I understand why, for purposes of edginess, we want Emmett Diggs to be killing white women. But what's still unanswered for me is how he becomes a killer in the first place. How does a man start out perfectly innocent and then turn into a person who's capable of murdering someone?"

. . .

Just as he is wondering how he will get inside, Emmett dis-covers that the back door is already open for him. And not just open, in fact, but missing. The back door is lying on the pantry floor, wrenched from its hinges, and if he's not careless he can walk right through the doorframe without getting splinters caught on the sleeve of his jacket.

. . .

She's showing no sign of letting go. "I have a gun," he tells her, no longer caring about his voice, and reaches behind his back to draw it from the waistband of his pants.

. . .

Ha! Does she look stupid? Not just nice but stupid? He makes a big show of going for his so-called gun and when he lifts up his arm to reach behind him she sees for the first time the tattoo running the length of his forearm, a long dark tattoo that looks as if it might be a blade or a sword, extending from the inside of his elbow to his wrist, a tribal-looking tattoo, abstract and arty, the sort of tattoo you'd find on someone working in a cheese shop.

. . .

The husband almost laughs at the stupidity of his own question. As soon as it's out of his mouth, he's already thinking, Um, let's see, where to begin: The legacy of Jim Crow? Mass incarceration? The criminal-justice system? Police brutality? Underemployment? White flight? Redlining? Profiling? Misrepresentation in the mass media? His first episode of network television: at least four to five million viewers will be tuning in. His first episode of network television: a weekly paycheck larger than he's ever seen, green envelopes with residual payments inside, Writers Guild health insurance for his wife and kid. His first episode of network television, and he doesn't want his mother and father to watch it.

. . .

"I have a gun." Emmett can hear more clearly now that he's inside the house. And emerging from the kitchen into the living room he sees them, and he thinks at first that they're dancing together, or maybe the boy is helping the woman lift something small but heavy. Their bodies are that kind of close. Her back is toward him, so that when the boy raises his fist he can't see what's happening on her face but he can see the boy's face and like a mirror it reflects his own bewilderment. The face asks, *What am I doing here?*

. . .

She was right. There is no gun. She knew it! Just as she knows that this whole big windup with his arm is silly. *Pow! Right in the kisser!* He can wave his fist around all he wants. See how he lets it hang there in midair, giving her an even better view of his tattoo. Nice try; he gets points for dramatic effect. *Bang! Zoom! To the moon, Alice!* She knows he's not going to do it.

. . .

Something is required of him in this moment, he knows. Someone is scared and needs his help. What's confusing is the question of who. Even though the boy is looming over her and has his fist cocked, they both look to him like they're in trouble.

. . .

Arm raised, hand clenched, he sees it then, clearly: she thinks he's a joke. He sees it in the stubborn way she holds her body, the blank look, the total absence of fear. *He's a lightweight. A joker. He's not going to do it.* Actually, he thinks, yes I am.

. . .

Bam! Pow! Right in the eye. She stumbles backward, nearly falling on her butt, letting go of the bag.

• • •

Lenny brightens. "Actually, I've been thinking about that! And here's where we can introduce some really dark, interesting stuff in the B story. You've seen *The Manchurian Candidate*, right? Okay, so what I'm thinking is: The warden has been doing some crazy psychological experiments on the inmates. Including Emmett Diggs. They've made him into an assassin and he doesn't even know it! Using, you know, radical brainwashing techniques, like a mixture of what they do in *A Clockwork Orange* plus electric shock therapy plus hypnosis? So what we come to realize is what triggers him is white women—" Abruptly the husband pushes away from the table, his chair squealing against the floor. He stands, rising to his full height, the sight of which makes Lenny pause and shoot a quick glance at the showrunner. "Everything okay, buddy?" the showrunner asks. The husband looks at him evenly. "Yes," he says. "I'm just getting a Coke."

• • •

There's more blood than he expected. The lady is holding her eye with the hand that was on the messenger bag, and he can see blood coming through her fingers. In her other hand she's still holding the telephone. The person on the other end seems to have finally hung up.

• • •

The husband walks right past the office kitchen and keeps heading down the hallway until he arrives at the elevator, which he takes to the lobby. After nodding at the security guard, he pushes through the glass doors. He stands on the empty sidewalk, squinting in the sunlight, barely registering the traffic going by. Then he slowly rotates to face the building. The security guard moves to open the door for him, but the husband shakes his head, pulls his car keys from his pocket, and turns toward the parking garage. The only place he wants to go right now is home.

. . .

Emmett hangs back for a moment, surveying the scene. On the one hand, he wants to go to the woman, who is sobbing in disbelief and dripping blood on the floor. But even though he has no way of knowing that a very good plastic surgeon will sew up her eyebrow with twenty-two stitches, or that her husband, despite his first show being canceled, will go on to write for a relatively popular supernatural police procedural, or that the woman, upon being asked by a female officer as they load her into the ambulance, "Now, were you in any other way assaulted?" will feel for the first time afraid, or that the dog, after attacking a UPS delivery driver, will be taken to a rescue organization up north that specializes in Australian shepherds, or that the daughter, having been told that her mother tripped at the gym and split her eyebrow open on a barbell, will grow nervous whenever the woman puts on exercise clothes—he somehow senses that regardless of the blood and tears his attention should be focused elsewhere. The sound of the front door opening softly makes him look at the boy (a little heavyset, still wearing the satchel slung over his shoulder), but before he can cross the room and reach him, before he can open his mouth and say, "Hey, brother," the boy has closed the door behind him and is gone.

JULIA AND SUNNY

Our friends, our very good friends, are getting a divorce. Julia and Sunny, lovable and loving, whom we've adored from the beginning, when we were all in medical school. The past few years have been difficult, we know that; we've known that for a while. It's not news to us that there've been problems, some counseling. A furnished short-term apartment. But still: it is a shock. Julia and Sunny, both in our wedding. And the same with us, for them. All those ski trips, the late-night card games, the time we hiked the Inca Trail and threw up repeatedly in the high altitude. There are kids now, and if any of us went in for that sort of thing, we'd be godparents; that's the kind of close we are. Or were? There are moments when we feel as if we don't know them anymore.

Julia's family owns property in New Hampshire, right on a lake, a place the four of us have been going to for so long that we can't help but think of it as ours. When we were in school it was close enough that we could go up anytime we wanted, but now with Julia and Sunny living in

Missouri and us in South Pasadena, it's no small feat to get there every summer, as we have. The third week of June, without fail.

It was at the lake house, two summers ago, that Julia began talking about letting some air into the relationship. Those were her words. She sat on the splintery bottom step, gnawing on a coffee stirrer and swatting at the blackflies, frowning, saying that she'd been depressed over the winter and started taking Lexapro. Lexapro? We tried not to let our eyes meet. Julia had always been so sparkly. And with all that energy! Loping off into the dawn, her orange nylon jacket bright in the mist. There was nothing she loved more than to run and swim, to travel impossible distances by bicycle, to sign up for half marathons on holiday weekends. She always wanted us to join her but never shamed us when we didn't. She never noticed when her running shoes tracked stuff all over the rug. But for an athletic person she was mystical too, full of superstitions and intuitive feelings. During our second-year exams, she brought each of us a little carved soapstone animal she'd found in a global-exchange gift shop behind the pizza parlor and insisted that we give them names. Hers, named Thug, looked as if it could have been a tapir. With the help of our animals we managed to pass our exams, to do well on them, in fact, and we celebrated by having a dance party and eating too much Ethiopian food and then, years and years later, felt unspeakably touched to discover Thug sitting on the windowsill of their guest bathroom, looking fine. That was Julia—sentimental and fond, likely to invest inanimate

objects with meaning, always sneaking off to exercise—
the Julia we knew, and it was hard to imagine that person
in the grip of a dark Midwestern winter, writing herself a
scrip for antianxiety meds. She tossed her chewed coffee
stirrer into the grass and said listlessly, "It'll biodegrade,
right?" When asked what she meant by *some air*, she sighed.
"I don't know. I'm still figuring that out."

Where was Sunny when she told us this? He must have
been off somewhere with the kids. It's easy to allow that
to happen: he's good with them, naturally, one of those
rare people who manages to still act like himself when he's
around them. Our son, Henry, has formed a strong attach-
ment to him, somewhat less so to their daughter, Coco,
who is eighteen months older and a little high-strung. They
don't always play well, so having Sunny there to facilitate
was helpful, maybe necessary. He kept them occupied with
owl droppings and games of Uno; he coated them in deet-
free bug spray and took them into the woods hunting for
edible plants that we then choked down as a bitter salad
with our dinner. Wherever he might have been with them
that afternoon, he wasn't at the house to add his thoughts
on letting the air in. Julia was the one who started us wondering, and for a long time afterward, hers would be the
only version we knew.

In a way, it was almost like being back at the beginning,
back before there was a Julia and Sunny, back when there
was just Julia, knocking tentatively at our apartment door,
bearing bagels and cream cheese, rustling in her workout
clothes, desperate to talk. She wanted to learn all she could

about Sunny, who had kissed her briefly on a back porch at a party, and as the people who usually sat next to him in immunology, we were interesting to her. Among the topics we covered were his note-taking, which was haphazard, his penmanship, loopy yet upright, the scuffed leather satchel in which he carried his books, the silver ring he wore on his right hand, the involuntary tapping of his foot. All three of us liked the dapper way he dressed, as if ready at a moment's notice to spend a day at the races. We liked, too, the things he'd say to us beneath his breath during the lecture, comments that were off-kilter and often very funny. He was easily the handsomest person in our class.

This was the point at which Julia would kick off her sneakers and we would really dig in. That woman Sheri—now what was that all about? Sunny had dated her at the very beginning of the year. She was a type that schools were eager to get their hands on back then: definitely not premed, but the kind who does something interdisciplinary, like East Asian studies, and then takes time off and has life experiences. In Sheri's case, she had doubled in classics and dance-theatre at Reed. She didn't have any piercings, at least as far as we could tell, but she did have a large tattoo on her right shoulder of a woman who looked suspiciously like her. Same flaming red hair, same wide red mouth. But how could we be sure? Asking would be rude. And she was difficult to have a conversation with, precise and cold in her way of speaking but nervous in her body, a little twitchy, her eyes darting about. Yet Sunny had wooed her, had undoubtedly slept with her! That haughty kook. At Halloween, they dressed up as a garbage collector and a bag of garbage. She was the hottest bag of garbage we'd ever seen, all silver duct tape and clinging black plastic, wobbling slightly in a pair of bondage boots. Soon after Halloween she and Sunny split up. "And a good thing too," we pointed out, given the accidental comedy of their names. Julia had never noticed this before, and now she laughed and laughed, with genuine delight. "Sunny and *Sher*-i," she repeated, eyes shining, and stretched her long limbs in the morning warmth of our apartment, already perfectly at home.

We liked it when Julia dropped in on us unannounced. She made us feel romantic. She'd peer at the photographs lined up along the mantel of the bricked-in fireplace; she'd compliment the ceramic salt and pepper shakers, shaped like French roosters, and open the flimsy kitchen cabinets to admire the plates and cups within. Settling back into the recently acquired club chair, our secret pride and joy, she propped her feet up on the matching ottoman and cried out, "I never want to sit in a papasan again!" It pleased us to no end. We were new to this, and sometimes just the sight of our clothes hanging companionably in the closet, or our large and small shoes jumbled in a heap by the door, would be enough to send us falling onto the nearest sofa in a sort of diabetic swoon. With Julia around, we wanted more than anything to while the day away discussing Sunny, and never have to send ourselves to the library, or to class.

Julia alone, whose soft knock on the door used to make us so happy, now fills us with a feeling similar to—we hate to say it—dread. Sometimes when she calls, we do not have the wherewithal to answer. We're afraid that the conversation will go on too long, or that she'll bring up Robert again and want to be affirmed. Sometimes we let her phone calls go straight to voice mail, and then allow a few days to pass before we even listen to the message.

"Aren't you going to call her back?"

"I think it's your turn. I'm pretty sure I did it last time."

"Are you keeping score?"

"Keeping track is not the same as keeping score."

"Seriously?"

"I just don't want this to become exclusively my job. Like what happened with the pool."

We can't help wishing that maybe one of these days Sunny would give us a call. Before we even really knew him we liked him, from afar we liked him, and sitting next to him in class we were charmed by his sudden way of smiling and his jaunty haircuts, which he received weekly from his octogenarian landlord, who in a former life had been not only a barber but a classical music deejay. This was the sort of information he'd occasionally divulge, each casually offered aside accreting into an ever more subtle, complex, and absorbing picture. He enjoyed reading fiction, especially Nordic detective novels. He'd once played soccer at a very high level, and done massive amounts of drugs. He'd gone to a good boarding school but a mediocre small college, spent much of his twenties trying to save his family's electronics business, and now here he was, making his comeback in medical school, where by all accounts but his own he was doing very well, with seemingly little effort.

We liked him, too, for not continuing to kiss Julia at parties. We appreciated the clarity of his intentions, and the way in which it flatteringly reflected our own: because what sane person wants to keep messing around at this age? That was what the undergraduate experience had been for, those four short and sweaty years. Now it was time to relax into something real. "He asked me on a *date*," Julia said in wonder. "That's actually the term he used." We suggested she wear her hair down.

She had brought over some different outfits to model for us. It was like watching a parade of past Julias: a kittenish little number she'd worn during her year singing a cappella; a pleated skirt and sweater set that had been her daily uniform as a temp. She retreated modestly into our bathroom between each costume change. "None of this is working, is it," she called from behind the door. We had a glass of wine waiting for her when she emerged again, plucking at the neckline of something cheap and brightly patterned, the kind of pretty dress found for half price on a sidewalk rack. She looked with longing at the wine but didn't take it.

"Will you drink it for me?" she asked. "Wine turns my teeth purple, so I'm just going to stick with gin and tonics for the night." She hiked up the skirt of her dress and climbed unceremoniously into the club chair. "Oh no. Do you think this place is going to have a full bar or just beer and wine?"

As we searched the bookshelf for our restaurant guide, Julia recounted tales of other boyfriends. She didn't want to make any of the same mistakes again. One ex had followed her down to Ecuador during her semester abroad and camped out for two weeks at a nearby youth hostel, watching her glumly from an internet café as she walked in the mornings to the local clinic. And then, the year after graduation, she had become embroiled with a Ph.D. student who was supposed to be supervising her at the lab where they worked, doing gene sequencing in a mild stupor. He was already engaged to someone else, which had made things extra heated and complicated between the two of them. She'd trained for her first marathon with him, and it was really more the running than the lab that had gotten them into trouble, and even though the relationship had ended in disaster and she was relieved, *glad*, that it was all over and done with, sometimes even now she found herself crying a little as she ran.

At least there was a full bar, according to our guide. "The crispy cod cakes come recommended. Also the short-rib ravioli."

"I'm not saying that going out to dinner automatically makes him a boyfriend. I'm getting ahead of myself. Way ahead of myself, as I have the tendency to do."

Sitting cross-legged in the chair, she planted her elbow on her knee, and then her chin on her palm. She gazed out the window at our air shaft, where the daylight was already starting to disappear. "Do you realize that Sunny is the first guy I've liked *before* he liked me?"

We stopped listening for a moment to wonder which of us had liked the other first, and how, when things happened so naturally and fast, it was possible to tell.

"Which seems significant somehow," she was saying. "Even if nothing comes of tonight, even if he never asks me on a date ever again. I'll still feel hopeful. In a general sense. About me and love." She inhaled. "Please forget I said that word." And then, recalling her audience, she smiled at us trustingly. "But you probably use it all the time."

We did, of course, and contrary to what we thought, it didn't necessarily make us authorities. We believed strongly and without any evidence that Sunny had liked her all along, even back in the days of Sheri and the garbage bags, and we told her so. From where our confidence came we couldn't have exactly said, but it struck us as indisputable, the rightness of Julia and Sunny, and on this feeling alone we were willing to stake our new friendship with her, and not to say a word when she leapt out of the chair and put on her coat while still wearing the cheap dress, which wasn't nearly nice enough for the restaurant where he was taking her. We experienced not the slightest protective urge as we sent her out the door.

In fact, the wrongness of the dress only served to further endear her to him, as did, we were to learn soon enough, her half-drunk insistence upon paying her share of the bill and her less-drunk attempt at getting him to sleep over. Julia had predicted correctly that he would never ask her on a date again. It seems miraculous to us now, the quantity of mistakes we all made, mistakes that should have sunk our romances straight off from the start: the hasty tumbling into bed, the disproportionate demands, the declaration of feelings. How did we manage to stay together despite all those offenses? Today young people are so *cagey*. Always keeping their options open, hedging their bets. Sure they have a lot of sex with near strangers, but that's not the same as being heedless in love. Not like us! Before we knew it, Sunny was making dinner for Julia most nights and cleaning up afterward. He was, he is, a terrific cook: cassoulets, curries, the most remarkably ungreasy fried chicken. We had never liked lentils before trying his. The card table set for four, the yellowish glow from Julia's thrift-store lamp, our textbooks, open to the same page, spread like stepping stones across the floor, the steam rising from whatever rich, soupy thing Sunny had just placed in front of us . . . It was a very sweet time.

Incredibly, he liked us back. That was the great, unhoped-for gift of it all, that Sunny—whom we had admired from both near and far, from our plastic seats in the lecture hall and over bagels at our apartment, who had so enchanted us with his distracting good looks and breezy style and eccentric remarks—appeared to find pleasure not only in her company but also in ours. It now seems negligible, his being six years older, but then the difference in age felt meaningful to us, as if we were being paid a serious compliment. Often, he would send us into spasms of private delight by doing that thing that comedians do, a callback, he was so good at doing that, plucking out of thin air some throwaway line we'd mentioned days earlier and then making it sound hilarious and intimate by referring to it again. He was listening, he was remembering! Even his impatience made us happy. Once, we were driving home from a camping trip in the mountains, and after sliding up and down the radio dial a few times, he finally landed on something he liked, turned up the volume, and then swiveled around to grin at us from the passenger seat. It was a song we hadn't heard before. Neither had Julia, clearly. She was driving with her eyes fastened on the road and a small, polite smile on her face. "Guys. Really?" Sunny looked at us in despair. "It's their best record. With the kudzu on the cover?" He let out a low groan. "You probably weren't eating solid foods yet."

So much of that is irretrievable now. The papers haven't been signed and filed yet, but Julia and Sunny, as a couple, are over. We've needed to keep reminding ourselves of this fact, only because it is so easy to slip into the habit of hoping otherwise. Our hope has remained quite stubborn for the most part.

"I met him at that physician wellness conference," Julia told us, and started to cry. This announcement occurred in Utah, about six months after our last time all together at the lake house. We were chopping things atop the kitchen's glittery granite counters while the children, stripped down to their long johns, watched television upstairs, and Sunny drove back to the grocery store because he was making turkey chili and the rental didn't have any cumin. His name was Robert, and he was in radiology. He lived in San Diego. His first email had just been friendly, Julia said. A regular old great-meeting-you-hope-our-paths-cross-again kind of email. No more than two sentences, and a signature featuring a long list of his various titles and affiliations. They had exchanged business cards after eating a complimentary buffet breakfast together at the hotel, at one of those big round banquet tables where solitary conference-goers are herded into each other's company. She had had a yogurt and watched him polish off a plate of warmed-over scrambled eggs. After the perfunctory exchange of cards, and after being slightly sickened by the spongy look of the eggs, she was then surprised to experience a little surge of erotic feeling when he stood from the table and she registered how tall he was. Not just tall, but big. Visibly strong through the chest and shoulders, and with thighs that looked like they could belong to an Olympic speed skater. Briefly he had loomed over her.

He was not her type at all, not by any stretch of the imagination—and yet she had been moved to reply. *Take care* was what he'd written in closing, and though every rational part of her knew that this farewell was, if not electronically generated, then at least his go-to phrase when signing off in casual correspondence, Julia couldn't help but feel that there was a hidden message for her in the words he had chosen, as if he had perceived, and was tactfully acknowledging, that she might be in need of some care. So it seemed reasonable to answer, *Thank you for your kind message*, and somehow just the typing of that one word, *kind*, released the series of sentences that followed, which began lightly enough, with a humorous account of the delays she had faced when flying home from the conference, but then made a sort of unexpected but lyrical turn toward the prospect of another long winter, the ineffectiveness of Lexapro, and the pain of watching one's only child struggle socially at school. Off it went, off into the ether, and a several-day silence had followed, long enough that she thought for certain she would never hear from him again, an idea that didn't really bother her once she realized that simply the act of writing those sentences down had helped her, and that maybe she should just start keeping a journal like everybody suggests, or at least consider combining some talk therapy with the medication, when bam! There in her inbox one overcast morning: the most wonderful, wonderful reply.

The sound of the garage door churning open caused us to drop our knives and circle helplessly around the kitchen, but Julia, pausing, promised us that Sunny already knew about the radiologist. "I'm committed to being transparent," she said. "And nothing has actually happened. I haven't even seen him since the conference, which is strange to realize. But I feel like something might happen. Soonish." She said it ominously, and all of a sudden looked as if she might cry again. She tore a paper towel from the roll and swabbed her eyes while we tried to keep our faces still. We wished that the children would appear, demanding snacks and a different show. What were we to do with this information, except pretend that we hadn't received it? Sunny came inside with the cumin, cheerfully unaware that we'd had this talk, and what a relief it was when Henry pulled his groin on the slopes the next day and we had to head home early.

Back in South Pasadena, under the safety of our own duvet, the conversation turned inevitably to Julia and Sunny. And now this new person, this Robert. A *radiologist*, of all things. It was impossible to conceive of the attraction, despite his size and his flair with email. The simple fact was that no one could compare to Sunny, who was sensitive without being spineless, capable but not controlling, funny, affectionate, generous, a highly respected doctor, a hands-on parent, and still so staggeringly handsome. He was aging better than the rest of us. True, they had landed in a city that was a bit off the beaten path, it was hard to get direct flights, the school options weren't terrific, he had persuaded her, for Coco's sake, to adopt a small hypoallergenic dog that she hadn't wanted, her father was showing signs of dementia—but still, on balance, in fact by all imaginable measures, her life was good. Wasn't it? We sank into bemused silence for a moment, and then got sidetracked by a disagreement over who had made the greater professional sacrifices for the other, Sunny or Julia, and in a fit of sulkiness stopped talking, only to wake up in the middle of the night to have intense, heartbroken sex that resulted in our sleeping through the alarm the next morning and Henry being late to Chinese school.

A phone call from Julia soon followed. "My mom wants Coco to stay with her over the summer. And though my initial response was to say no, now I'm thinking it could be good for both of them." She was calling from the car, on her way home from the hospital. "Coco can be an uplifting presence when she wants to be. Even if she's not, just her being there will keep Mom from dwelling and, you know, fixating. She was always a worrier but it's gotten so much worse with my dad." The ticking of a turn signal punctuated the roar in the background. "The great thing is it'll be a chance for Coco to train with my old swim coach. And she's never ready to come home when we visit. She always wants to stay longer. I think she's kind of starved for an environment that isn't dominated by freeways and Chipotles. A place where you can walk to the corner drugstore." Julia's parents live for most of the year in Rhode Island, in one of those flat-faced colonial houses that stand a little too close to the road. "Does it sound like I'm rationalizing? I'm really not. I really think this will be beneficial for everyone. It's an adventure for Coco, and it gives us a little space. A little room to breathe. Do you realize that Sunny and I have not taken a single vacation without her since the day she was born? I know—you're the same as us. I don't need to tell you. And I know it seems easier with just the one to bring them everywhere, especially when they're this age and they're good travelers, but it's actually not easier in the end, it takes its toll, and we have to remember how important it is, to have time alone as adults—" A getaway! Just the two of them and their swimsuits. It was exactly what they needed. The Azores, or Indonesia . . . "Well, what I meant was time *alone* alone, not together alone," she said gently. "Sunny has signed up for a cruise, believe it or not, because he's short on his CME credits. Then he'll stay on in Alaska for a few weeks to see the fjords and do some camping. You know how he gets about *Grizzly Man*. It's still his favorite." And what would she do? All by herself? With that long luxurious stretch of unencumbered time? It felt dangerous to ask. "Oh, I'm staying put. Cranking up the air as high as I want and working some extra weekends. Someone has to be here with Peaches."

There was no mention of Robert. And no mention, conspicuously, of the lake house. Months later, in a semi-apologetic text, it was confirmed that we wouldn't be gathering there in June. But we have managed to get together with Julia twice this year: first at a Houston's off the 405 in Irvine, roughly equidistant between San Diego and our house, and the second time, also in Orange County oddly enough, for a long, hot, glazed-over day at Disneyland with the kids.

We should acknowledge that Robert ended up not being as bad as we thought he would be. The meeting up at Houston's had been his idea, according to Julia, and as we drove south we couldn't decide whether this choice was considerate on his part, our drive being moderately shorter than theirs, or whether it implied a sort of finicky exactness, an insistence on making everything "fair" instead of just sucking it up and driving to South Pasadena as Julia had most likely wanted. But maybe Robert's plan suggested depths of sensitivity that we hadn't expected, allowing him to intuit that we weren't yet ready to have him hanging out at our house, his very presence polluting the home in which Sunny had cooked countless pots of dal and relinquished so many hands of hearts. And the fact is, we were not ready, not at all. Which was nice of him to pick up on. Then again, if he'd really been sensitive, he would have suggested the Houston's that was less than three miles away from us.

Once we all got settled in the leather booth, it became clear that Robert knew the menu extremely well; without even needing to look at it, he ordered the spinach dip and cheese bread and grilled artichokes for the table. When we asked for margaritas, we learned that he was sober. "Three years and eight months," he said with simple happiness. It was hard to reconcile this large, ruddy person with the radiologist we'd imagined, the bloodless Lothario who had destroyed our friends' marriage. As much effort as we had put into hating him over the past many months, regularly enraged by the thought of him, our insides roiling at the sound of his name, Robert was, we had to admit, probably beside the point. We protested a little when he reached for the check, but eventually gave in and said thank you. He and Julia had been careful to leave a few inches of space between them throughout dinner, and as we watched them cross the parking lot, we saw her take his hand and kiss it.

The more recent trip to Disneyland was, on the whole, less successful. Julia had talked Coco into trying a weeklong marine biology camp on Catalina Island, and apparently her reward for surviving it was a weekend at the "Happiest

Place on Earth": the proximity of all this to San Diego was not lost on us. But it had been such a long time since the kids had seen each other. We didn't want to take the high road at the expense of Henry, who'd been lobbying to do the Jedi Training Academy for a while now, and despite our discomfort with Julia's self-interested itinerary, and some queasiness with respect to the Disney empire, there was no graceful way to avoid going. And we should say up front that the bulk of the blame for what happened at the end of the day falls squarely on us.

The real problem was the lack of Sunny, of course—we hadn't sufficiently prepared Henry for the shock of this— we'd mentioned it plenty of times on the drive to Anaheim, but the reality of Sunny not being with us was a different thing altogether. Without Sunny around, the full extent of our children's incompatibility was free to reveal itself: Coco wanting to do nothing but get her autograph book signed and have her photo taken with princess reenactors, Henry gloomy and lagging behind, unable to recover from the brief high of being a Jedi trainee, which had required us to register as soon as the park opened and then lasted all of twenty minutes. Their only shared inclination was to ask wistfully for "mementos" while stopping to examine the merchandise at gift shops. Neither of them seemed particularly interested in the rides; both of them were unsatisfied with the food options. All of us felt somewhat stunned by the heat and the long waits in line. None of this was helped by the fact that Coco had shot up in the past year and now towered incongruously over Henry.

While shuffling slowly forward we tried to ask Coco questions about her time on Catalina, but she offered only vague, incomplete answers, made more difficult to understand by a metal appliance that had been installed inside the roof of her mouth. "It's called a palatal crib," Julia murmured. "I know it looks like a medieval torture device, but there was no other way to stop her." Coco was a hardened thumb-sucker, grown furtive and resourceful over the years. "The orthodontist said that we couldn't even think about braces until we achieved 'total extinction of the habit.'" She widened her eyes at the terminology. "We had to do something—Sunny felt the same way."

We must have perked up at the reference because Julia stopped talking about the crib and instead continued warmly on the subject of Sunny. "I mean I knew this before, obviously, but he is an incredible co-parent. That hasn't changed a bit. We are completely in sync when it comes to Coco. Completely on the same page in terms of making this transition feel okay for her. We have dinner as a family now three nights a week, which is actually more often than when we were still living together." She wasn't bothering to speak in a lowered voice anymore, and Coco seemed undisturbed by the topic, staring agreeably into space, as if she was already accustomed to hearing it discussed in her vicinity.

"And she and Robert," we asked, "they're hitting it off? That's going well?" Julia's lovely face froze into an expression of pure alarm just as Coco, without missing a beat, asked—in a perfectly distinct, piping voice—"Who's Robert?"

"He's a colleague, baby," she said, "you haven't met him yet," and from her backpack she handed out sticks of mint gum to all except Coco, with her mouth crib, who received an energy bar instead. We chewed in silence. No subtle means of changing the subject came immediately to mind. "Watch where you're stepping," Julia warned as she steered the children around a pat of bright pink bubblegum glistening on the ground. "That is definitely not sugarless," Coco noted, and then craned her neck to see if she could guess which person in front of us had spit it out.

But as awful as that moment had been, it wasn't as bad as what we felt later that night, after we had dropped off Coco and Julia at their Disneyland-adjacent hotel, and after we had made the trek back to South Pasadena and pulled into our driveway. We turned around and there in the back seat was Henry, sound asleep: head cocked and mouth gaping, arms spread in surrender, a lightsaber in one hand and a small square of silky, pale blue material in the other. Oh God. We knew immediately what it was. We would know that silky scrap anywhere. It was Coco's. It had started out years earlier as the satin trim on a fancy chenille baby blanket, a blanket she had loved, her favorite thing to do with this blanket being to pile it up on one side of her and then take the very tip of its corner and press it against her nose, where she would stroke it voluptuously with an index finger as she sucked on her then-permissible thumb. Without the blanket she refused to go to sleep; also, she refused to read or be read to, watch a movie, take a time-out, ride in the car—and each summer at the lake house, when Coco emerged from the back of the Subaru, the blanket would appear a little further diminished—until at last it had disintegrated into this one remaining relic-like bit of trim, no more than three inches square. For a few long minutes we sat there in the driveway staring at Henry, feeling both furious and sort of sympathetic that he was acting out in this weird way.

When questioned the next morning, he was not very forthcoming.

How did he end up with Coco's wubby?

She was playing with it when we drove them back to the hotel.

But how did it come to be in his possession?

She put it in the cup holder when Julia told her to pull her sweater from her backpack.

And after she put it in the cup holder?

They got out of the car.

Didn't he tell Coco that she'd forgotten her lanyard, and hand it to her?

Yes.

So why didn't he tell her that she'd left her wubby in the cup holder?

He'd forgotten to mention it.

Doesn't he know how much it means to her?

At this, Henry merely shrugged. He was glowing with resentment and by now crying hard. We discussed the logistics of driving to Anaheim and catching Julia before she left the hotel for the airport, but soon enough came to our senses and made Henry draw a card, first in pencil and then more carefully in pen, which we enclosed in a self-sealing business envelope, unable to find anything cuter, along with the little blue remnant. While it wouldn't quite beat them back to Missouri, Coco would be reunited with her transitional object in just a matter of days. So what an unwelcome surprise it was when the business envelope and its contents appeared in our mailbox several weeks later, looking battered. How stupid—the wrong address! But to us it was the right address, and would always be the right address: the house to which, for years, we had sent holiday popcorn tins and joke gifts and small belated offerings to mark Coco's birthdays. There were now two new addresses, though still in the same zip code, and we hadn't had the chance to update our contacts list with either.

It goes without saying that we did repackage the whole thing, making sure to write down Julia's new house number and street and also including a set of flavored lip balms designed to look like macarons, which was meant as a mea culpa to Coco but which also necessitated a larger, padded envelope and a trip to the post office in order for it to be weighed and affixed with the correct postage. Little did we know that due to operating budget shortfalls, the post office now closes early on Saturdays—so the padded envelope went into the back seat of the car, and then it migrated to the trunk when Henry and his friends Noah and Griffin had to be driven to basketball practice, and there it stayed for quite a while until a long-overdue Costco haul, when it was discovered again and placed inside the capacious French shoulder bag that's intended to collapse into chic origami but, as the repository for seemingly all of the family's cough drop wrappers, parking tickets, reusable water bottles, school newsletters, store receipts, etc., is never empty enough to do so.

An absurdly long delay—but we did keep Julia posted on our efforts and having looked hard at ourselves can say that it truly was a case of two parents working full-time, a kitchen remodel going sideways, their kid trying out for the travel team and actually making it, and life just being the breathless, nonstop, three-ring circus that it tends to be these days. After a month of being toted about in the bag, the envelope became part of the furniture, as they say, and encountering its puffy presence while fishing around for a permission slip or the car keys came to feel sort of reassuring. In fact, the envelope was still inside the French shoulder bag when a last-minute trip to New York proved unavoidable, a parent's knee finally needing to be replaced, and who of all people should materialize at the Muji store near the food court in JFK's Terminal 5—full head of hair appearing above the rows of tiny Japanese containers, lean frame moving down the aisle—but Sunny. Our Sunny. Wearing a slate-gray coat and a bright, beautifully striped scarf, looking as marvelous as ever.

It felt unbelievably good to hug him. He smelled of coffee and fig shampoo. Both the scarf and the coat were cashmere, and though it's possible that he had an extra layer on underneath the coat, he didn't feel as thin as we'd been worried he might be. Inexplicably, he seemed an inch or so taller. Never before had my head fit so neatly under his chin. I must have held on for a second too long because he gave me a little pat on the back, letting go.

He was coming from Glasgow, of all places, where he'd been invited to give a talk. He said it went well, and that he'd been traveling more in general. Gracious as always, he asked after us, after Henry in particular, inquiring about school, the basketball season, whether he was still interested in Houdini. He laughed when he learned about Henry's ongoing efforts to raise enough money to buy a straitjacket. As we talked, we browsed through the selection of soothing organizational items, unable to stop touching things and weighing them in our hands, and I chattered about the knee replacement and holiday plans and staffing changes at the hospital, trying to resist the urge to hug him again. It was just so good to see him. It had been such a long time, and he looked so exactly himself, which was a relief to me, a great comfort and a relief. Finally, I admitted this aloud and pressed my face against his shoulder, adding how glad I was to hear that they were all doing so well. Sunny turned to look at me. "We are?" His surprise seemed real. He picked up a pocket notebook and began thumbing through its pages. "Julia told you that?" He shook his head. Then he smiled crookedly at the notebook. "I think it's safe to say that she's speaking for herself."

The notebook ended up going back on the shelf but he did hold on to a clever stapler and hovered over the rainbow array of gel pens, asking if I thought Coco would like them. His question reminded me, for obvious reasons, of the package I had been carrying around with me all this time, the package addressed to Coco; I dug it out of my shoulder bag and held it up for him to see. As soon as I did so, I felt ashamed that we had used Julia's address and not his. Yet it somehow seemed not only a fitting correction but an act of fate that he should be the one to deliver it. I imagined the look of amazement on her face when her father walked through the door, bearing his prize: I could picture the appliance glinting in her slightly opened mouth. What serendipity that I hadn't had the chance to make a second trip to the post office! For once I felt good about being harried. I gave the padded envelope to Sunny and explained what was inside.

"Disneyland," he echoed, and then realized: "Which was in August."

I didn't want to bore him with the convoluted story. He had a flight to catch, and still another one after that before he reached home. I knew from experience that he didn't like to rush. He seemed to have changed his mind about the stapler and the pens, maybe because a short line had formed at the register or maybe because—this was my pleased, ridiculous thought in the moment—he already had something special to bring back to her. Outside the store we hugged once more, and this time Sunny was the one to give an extra-long squeeze, and the last thing he said was "Be sure to tell Henry I said hey," before he adjusted the beautiful scarf and headed for his gate.

In other words, we ended on a very warm note, and I turned dreamily in the direction of my own gate, still glowing from the encounter with Sunny but already starting to feel a familiar melancholy at the thought of their divorce. The truth is that my sense of loss has not abated, as I originally believed it might, with the passing of time. *Tincture of time*—a phrase I had first heard while sitting beside Sunny in immunology, his foot tapping away. I think it was my sadness that made me glance over my shoulder to steal one more look at his gray coat, growing smaller as he retreated down the bright, polished corridor, and this was how I happened to see what he did then, which was to take the padded envelope from under his arm and drop it into a large putty-colored trash receptacle. He did it without stopping, in one swift motion, a gesture so fluid that I almost missed it. But this was unmistakably what he did.

Of course I was surprised, actually quite shaken, and I spent the flight home flipping from one free movie to another and trying to analyze the act that I'd not been meant to see. My first hopeful thought was that Sunny didn't want to reintroduce a crutch after Coco had learned to live without it. Entirely possible. Less probable but also consoling was the idea that he objected to the artificial additives in flavored lip balm—I had mentioned the little gift we'd included—or the marketing of beauty products to preadolescent girls. Maybe he'd never liked the blanket and was just as glad to have it gone. Maybe he was mad at Julia for allowing it to get lost. Gradually, though, my thinking grew darker, and on the drive home from LAX to South Pasadena, I find myself wondering if his treatment of the envelope might be a reflection of how he feels about us.

It's well after eleven when I pull up to the house. They've left the lights on for me, but my first impulse upon stepping inside is to turn them off. Upstairs they are in their rooms, asleep, which makes the house feel very still but also full. In the darkened living room, I pick my way to the club chair, now twice reupholstered, and as I sit down, it occurs to me that though I will certainly describe running into Sunny, I'll keep the other part of what I saw to myself. Now that I'm home it's clear that there is no need, really, to bring this abrasive bit of mystery in through the door with me.

Our months of conjecture, our lengthy, circular conversations with Julia: they have left us exhausted, not to mention irritable with each other, and with no deeper understanding of why she doesn't love Sunny in the same way she used to. We ask ourselves, Is there something she isn't telling us? Is she protecting us, out of kindness, from disturbing truths—about Sunny? Or herself? As much as we try, we can't bring ourselves to believe what she keeps insisting on, which is simply that she wasn't happy. Simply that her feelings changed. Because this is inconceivable to us, when ours have remained so constant. We love them, Sunny and Julia, as much as we did in the beginning.

Sometimes it happens that in the early morning, we shuffle out onto the landing at the same time—my snoring has gotten worse, so lately I've been sleeping in the guest room—and without speaking we keep shuffling forward until we're touching, resting on the other's upright body, and almost magically, Henry opens up the door to his bedroom, and out he shuffles too. The three of us lean into one another, and it's not exactly a group hug but more like the kind of huddling that animals do in the cold, our flanks rising and falling with our breaths. We stand there sleepily for a minute or two, and once in a while, I'll think I smell something faint and intoxicating, similar to the fancy shampoo that Sunny must have used at his Glasgow hotel; I'll sniff Henry's hair, sink my nose into my husband's T-shirt, trying without success to find it again. Then, as easily as we came together, we break apart and go about our business, knowing that soon we'll be bumping up against the same bodies, whether on the landing or in the kitchen or somewhere else. Knowing that, it seems to me, is enough. And not just enough, but plenty.

LIKES

The dad scrolled through his daughter's Instagram account, looking for clues. The most recent post was a photograph of an ice cream cone, extravagantly large, held up against a white wall by a disembodied hand. Peppermint stick, or strawberry. The mound was starting to melt, a trickle of it inching down the cone and drawing dangerously close to the thumb. His daughter's.

The next photo was a close-up of a shop window. Inside the window glowed a pink neon sign spelling out the word *warm* in lowercase letters. The glowing word took up most of the frame: it was impossible to tell what sort of store it was.

Another close-up: an eraser-colored rose, its petals halfway unfurled.

A panorama: the sky at sunset.

A shot of her dog, Bob, curled up like a cinnamon bun on the pleated, peachy expanse of her bed.

And then an earlobe—was that what it was? Soft, rounded, partly in shadow.

He closed his eyes and put down the phone.

His daughter was nearly twelve, and difficult to talk to.

. . .

Normally she rode the bus home from school, but now that she had to do physical therapy twice a week, he had been picking her up and taking her to the appointments. He felt responsible. These problems with her joints—runner's knee, Achilles tendinitis—were undoubtedly a handicap she'd inherited from his gouty side of the family. In ballet class, she could no longer do grand pliés or go up to relevé. In the middle of the night, she would wake up in pain. He kept a tin of Tiger Balm on her nightstand so that she could find it easily in the dark.

The physical therapist was a young woman dressed as an older one, in ironed slacks and support shoes. She had a secretive smile and a stiff demeanor. The dad didn't always feel comfortable asking her questions, but his daughter seemed to like her. "Hi, Ivy," the therapist would murmur as they entered the office, her little smile widening, and the two of them would disappear into the equipment. From the waiting room, the dad could hear the whir of the stationary bicycle and the sound of their voices, his silent companion from the car suddenly talkative. It made a kind of music, the wheel spinning and her talking.

. . .

Correction: his daughter wasn't entirely silent in the car. She sang along to songs on the radio, songs patchy with blanked-out words that she made a point of mouthing but didn't say aloud. A billboard might prompt her to ask a question like *Why is she drinking out of a paper bag?* Sometimes, gazing at her phone, she would let out a low, triumphant hiss. *Yesssss!* She'd got every answer right on the Kylie Jenner quiz. Received seventy-four likes on her ice cream photo. Set a new personal record on her Snapchat streak with Talia. Other days her phone lay inert in her lap. Only last week she had asked, eyes brimming and fixed on the dashboard, "Dad, can I be homeschooled?" Undone, he'd answered, "Sure."

• • •

After physical therapy, in the elevator heading down to the parking lot, he gave her a squeeze and said, "You're quite the conversationalist in there." His daughter looked at him with alarm. Of course it hadn't come out the way he'd wanted it to. "I'm glad," he tried again, "that there's an adult you enjoy talking to." Which was true, although it sounded as if he meant the opposite. Even to his own ears he sounded sorry for himself. But his daughter, good for her, was not thinking about him or his feelings. She stared at the elevator doors. "You're making me feel like I talk too much!" she whispered furiously, deep in her own embarrassment.

• • •

New Instagram post: a peeled-off pair of ballet tights, splayed on the white tiles of a bathroom floor.

• • •

Some days his daughter's quietness in the car felt blank and mysterious; but some days it felt excruciatingly full, like an inflamed internal organ about to burst. On one such afternoon the dad said carefully, "I'm not going to look at you. I'm not going to say anything. I'm just going to keep my eyes on the road. I'm going to keep driving, and, when you're ready, you say whatever you want." After a moment of silence, she said, "I'm considering it." And then, "Can I curse?" He nodded. She asked, "You won't make any noises, or have any expressions at all on your face?" He nodded again. They drove for several more minutes. The effort was killing him. Also the dread. He wasn't sure if he had the capacity to receive whatever feeling it was that she was full of. When they were only three blocks from the therapist's office, she said to the windshield, "I have no friends." As he eased into the parking lot, she said, "And don't tell me, 'But you were just at Annie's house last Friday.' I know that's what you're going to say. But you can't make me feel better. People only hang out with me because there's nobody else around. I'm not their friend." She opened the car door slowly. "I'm their second choice." She heaved her backpack off the floor while he stayed behind the wheel, noticing his breath and absorbing the punch in various parts of his body. Why hadn't she cursed?

. . .

New post: a hamburger with lettuce and Thousand Island dressing, cut in half, cooked medium rare.

. . .

The physical therapist recommended a series of exercises to do at home. Some, like the calf raises, were straightforward, but others had names such as Clam. Studying the printout, with its unhelpful black-and-white drawings, the dad asked, "You understand what all of this means?" Fire Hydrant. Dipping Bird. Short Bridge. Clock. His daughter didn't glance up from her phone: "Uh-huh." He stuck the paper to the refrigerator with a magnet. It looked somewhat quaint there. All her handouts from school were now distributed digitally, for environmental reasons. "You know you're supposed to be doing these every night?" No answer. Marooned on one side of the island, he wondered, not for the first time, if open concept was such a great thing after all. Was she in the kitchen talking with him, or was she in the family room, on the sofa with her phone? Unclear. Without untying the laces, she scraped off her sneakers, toe to heel. Two consecutive thunks. "Your recovery depends on it. You know that, right?" Elegantly, she lifted her long legs up and out of sight. "Ivy?" She sank beneath the horizon of the sofa. "Hello?"

. . .

Guess what: her only homework was to watch TV. This was what his daughter announced when he picked her up from ballet class. In a series of texts, he and his wife agreed that they would order ramen and watch the presidential debate as a family, and though it took them a while to get settled—the restaurant had sent only one spicy instead of two, and when they sat down on the sofa Bob kept jumping into their laps and had to be crated—once they finally organized themselves, with their drinks and their bowls and their napkins and their chopsticks, it felt warm and momentous being there together in front of the television. Dorothy muttered encouragement at the moderator. "Keep at him," she said, bent over her noodles. "Keep the pressure on!"

As long as Dorothy was leaning forward, he could now and then steal a sideways glance at his daughter. She appeared to be paying attention, her eyes slightly widened and her bowl sitting neglected on the coffee table. Then suddenly she leapt off the sofa and ran upstairs.

"You all right?" he called. "Ivy?"

"It's making me uncomfortable!" she yelled from the top of the staircase. He could picture her standing there, one foot raised, ready to flee. "Tell me when this part is over, okay?"

He wanted to share a commiserating look with Dorothy, but she was still watching the screen, sawing her little pendant back and forth on its chain. "So much for current events," he said.

. . .

His daughter had a pretty collection of pens and pencils. A tiny roll of tape, a pink pocket stapler, and a packet of candy-colored paper clips. All these items lived inside a sleek gold pouch with a zipper, and were brought out into the open when she was doing her homework at the kitchen table. Her tapered fingers danced over them in search of the right highlighter. Her fingernails sparkled. Her school supplies sparkled. She had affixed very small puffy stickers in strategic places to her notebooks and binders. Watching her at work, he realized with pride that his daughter would have been one of those girls who intimidated him when he was that age.

When he was that age! A slight prickling, like sensation restoring itself to a numb hand. Was his old self considering a return? To his surprise, he had trouble recalling his thoughts and emotions from sixth grade. Surprising, because he remembered the *fact* of having felt things; it was the point at which his parents took to calling him Heathcliff.

There were a few standouts, to be sure—the memory of being lifted into the air and carried on a gurney, after he'd badly sprained his ankle on the basketball court, and noticing how far away the ceiling of the gym appeared, and the menacing pattern of the rafters—but, in terms of day-to-day twelve-year-old feelings, he had, strangely, lost access. And the access needed to be only temporary: all he wanted was a point of comparison. Was what she was going through *normal*? In the afternoons he held his breath, never knowing which girl was going to climb into the passenger seat: the happy one, braces flashing, asking if they could make a really quick stop at Baskin-Robbins; or the other one, the one in pain. Had he ever felt that way, too? If only he could remember. All that came to him were the first and last names, in no particular order, of every kid in his homeroom: Steven Burke, Tracy Mayson, Derek Wong, Billy Flanagan, Dawn Littlejohn, Josh Tokofsky, Luke Mandel,

Rafi Moncho, Danielle Blood . . . And sometimes along
with the names the faces would materialize, like mug shots.

. . .

New post: a pair of lips, shining wetly.

. . .

"Try not to internalize," Dorothy whispered to him, taking his hand as they waited in the dank hallway outside
the *Nutcracker* auditions. "Practice wearing a neutral expression." They stood in silence for a while, trying to hear
what was going on behind the closed doors. When their
daughter finally exited, looking a little dazed, they gently
shepherded her to the car. Did she want lunch? Starbucks?
"If it's okay, I think I'd just like to go home and watch You-
Tube," she said quietly.

. . .

From the depths of the sofa, a now familiar voice bubbled:
"Hi, guys! I'm back, and I'm so excited because today I'm
going to be talking about room decor. As you guys know, I
love being creative when it comes to doing DIY decor, but
today is extra special because I'm going to be showing you
my mini HomeGoods haul! I got so many amazing things,
but I think the thing that I love the most is this incredibly
fluffy pillow—as you can see, it's huge, and I'm pretty sure
it's real sheepskin. Yeah, it says here 100 percent wool from
New Zealand, but don't worry, no sheep were killed or anything—I don't think so, right? It'll just grow back. But the

best part is how good it goes with these other decorative pillows I got at HomeGoods—that place is so amazing! Their selection is always changing! I went in thinking I needed picture frames and a dog bed but then I turned down this one aisle and I saw the pillows and I went crazy!"

. . .

By nightfall his daughter seemed to have revived. She practiced her jazz turns on the slick floor of the kitchen; she winked and dimpled at her reflection in the sliding doors, as if for an audience stretching into the darkened backyard. The dad, rinsing dishes in the sink, had to keep dodging her left foot, which she kicked, without warning, high into the air. She always kicked on that side; it was naturally the more flexible of the two. To the dad, it would have made more sense to practice kicking on the *less* stretchy side. *I am the best*, she sang tunelessly, *the best, the best, the best. You can't beat me, no you can't, so don't even try, because I am the best.* The song sounded as if it had been made up on the spot.

. . .

Later that week, the physical therapist came into the waiting room while his daughter was still whirring away on the bicycle. For a moment, he thought she was there to grab a magazine, but then she perched on the chair beside him and started speaking. "I'm wondering," she said, wearing her small, formal smile, "if Ivy has been keeping up with her exercises at home?" His chest began to tingle, the Ivy-vise squeezing. She wasn't improving. She wasn't going to get a decent part in *The Nutcracker*. She'd have to spend a second year in the angel corps, shuffling across the stage in the Snowflake scene while holding a battery-operated candle from Home Depot. He felt totally defeated. "I think she has," he said. "I've been telling her to." Then he admitted, "But I really don't know." To his shame, he heard himself adding, somewhat sulkily, "Maybe you should ask her."

• • •

Another not-great day at school. His daughter buried her chin and mouth into the folds of her scarf and stared unseeingly at the road, not bothering to change the radio station. Election coverage continued unchecked in the background. Beyond the windshield, a vapor trail bisected the blue sky. Closer to the ground, block after block of residential development streamed past. As they merged onto the highway, she asked, "Do *you* think I cry too much?" He sat with the question for a handful of seconds and then inquired, evenly, "Who told you that?" When she didn't answer, he asked, a little less evenly, "Who said that bullshit to you?" Also, "When did it become a crime to *feel* things?" She retreated deeper into her scarf. "Oh, God, Dad. Forget I asked. It doesn't matter," and he glanced down at the insulated cup resting in the holder between them. That fucking coffee! He'd been suckered by the promised ease of "drive-thru" and ended up arriving ten minutes late for pickup. Only ten minutes, not even a quarter of an hour, but long enough for someone to have said something awful to her.

If that indeed was what had happened. Who knew what really went on in the cluster of low-slung buildings that she disappeared into and emerged from every day? He had the urge to carry her far away from them, as far as possible. The value of peer interaction was definitely overstated. He could fill the tank, surprise Dorothy at work, load the trunk with nonperishable groceries and supplies, and then it'd be just the three of them, the open road. Not like free spirits, exactly, more like refugees from the zombie apocalypse, but, still, they'd be together. Plus Bob. He'd almost forgotten the dog.

. . .

New post: a cupcake, frosted to look like the cute face of a pig.

. . .

In late October, unexpectedly, a stretch of sunshine. First off, she'd been cast as a dragon dancer in the Chinese Tea scene, and even though only the lower half of her would be visible, she was coming home from the rehearsals in high spirits. Which she attributed to teamwork, telling him, "You see, it *is* like playing a sport." And then, in the space of a few days: an Evite to a disco-themed murder-mystery party; an afternoon working with her partner on a social studies project that turned into a movie night and a sleepover; a plan to go with three girls from her Girl Scout troop to the outlet mall. The dad stood on the front walkway and watched her slide into the back seat of the troop mother's minivan; as it pulled away from the curb, he waved to the shadowy parent behind the wheel. Their neighbor Marcia happened to be dragging in her trash cans. He waved at her, too. "I can't believe how big she's getting!" Marcia called. "Tell me about it," he said. "Always running off somewhere. I can't keep up!" He knew he sounded like an ass but he couldn't help it. He floated up the walkway and in through the front door, and finding Dorothy upstairs, shaking out the bedcovers, he hugged her from behind and made her topple over.

. . .

On Tuesday, the physical therapist greeted them as usual. "Hi, Ivy," she said through her little smile, as if he were merely the hulking, nameless attendant who traveled alongside the patient. But today it didn't bother him, because right away he saw that she had done her duty and voted. He pointed to the oblong sticker on the breast pocket of her gray grown-up-looking blouse, and then pointed to the same sticker attached to his own chest. Earlier, he had debated whether he should wait until after school and take his daughter with him—it'd be something that she could tell *her* daughter about, had been his thinking—but then he remembered that she had therapy and during his lunch hour went ahead on his own to the polling station, which was in the cavernous basement of an Armenian church. After pointing to their matching stickers, he gave the physical therapist a grin and a thumbs-up. Uncharacteristically, she returned the gesture with open enthusiasm. Oho! Maybe he'd stumbled upon the best way to communicate with her—through hand signals. He swelled suddenly with positive feelings for her. This competent young woman, who was helping his daughter; those nice Armenian congregants who volunteered for long shifts at the polls; the sensible, civic-minded men and women who patiently waited with him, giving up their lunch hours as he had—he felt good about them. He felt good about humanity in general. Basic decency would prevail, and this exhausting, insane election season would soon be over, and by tomorrow he could commit his energies fully to planning the Thanksgiving menu and making sure that his daughter did her Fire Hydrants every night and got better.

. . .

New post: a black square. Not a photo of a black square but a photo of total blackness. As if the camera had misfired, or the film had been accidentally exposed.

. . .

The whole family had a hard time getting up the next morning. The dad felt as if he had been run over by a truck, a big shiny pickup truck that had come swerving out of the darkness and mowed him down, and now had backed up and was waiting for him, its engine revving. His daughter crouched by his pillow and asked, as she often did, "Do I have to go to school today?" Her eyes had turned narrow from crying, then sleeping; her nightshirt had a silvery unicorn on it. They had let her stay up to watch the results with them, and even in the dim light she looked haggard. "No," he said, placing the pillow over his head. "Go back to sleep." It was what he intended to do. He had a very small window in which he could slip back into unconsciousness and then wake up in a world where the election hadn't happened. He tried the trick he'd developed after the first of several basketball injuries, the trick where he would slow his breathing and lie perfectly still, and the throbbing in his ankle would cease, and he could fool himself into believing that he was strong and well before finally relaxing into sleep. He imagined himself in his old bedroom, on his single bed, wearing nothing but his Celtics shorts. He repeated to himself, *Fit as a fiddle. Fit as a fiddle.* But he was agonizingly awake. Dorothy's body heat beside him was throwing him off. He pushed away the pillow and sighed, and was startled to see his daughter standing in the doorway, fully dressed, with her backpack on. "What are you doing?" he groaned. "Why aren't you in bed?" She took a nervous step backward. "Daddy," she said. "I thought you were joking."

. . .

Life was a subject on which his daughter collected inspirational quotes. Her favorite—"Life always offers you a second chance. It's called tomorrow"—served as the bio on her Instagram profile. If asked to describe herself, she invariably said either "fantabulous" or "optimistic." Among the many items on the third draft of her Christmas list was something called a Happiness Planner, a daily journal designed, she explained, to create positive thinking and personal growth. Christmas was well over a month away, though nearly all the houses on the block already had their lights up.

On a cold morning, the dad sank into the driver's seat, and in a fog he backed the car down the driveway and into the street before he became aware of a painted wooden sign on top of his dashboard. It was long and thin, with a black background and italicized gold lettering; the paint had been deliberately rubbed away from the sign's edges to make it look like an heirloom that had once hung in an ancestor's homestead. Usually this sign hung on the wall above his daughter's bed, for the most part unnoticed by him, but now, looking at it closely, he saw that its syntax was slightly garbled. It read, *Life is always offered a second chance. It's called tomorrow.* Not as bad as what he'd seen in some instruction manuals, but still off, and annoyingly so, considering that the words were the whole point. He flipped over the sign to confirm his suspicions about where it had been manufactured. *Proudly made in Michigan, USA,* the sticker said. China was off the hook! He didn't know why he bothered feeling surprised anymore. He tossed the sign into the back seat, facedown. It struck him as darkly symbolic, as so many things did these days. Impersonal *life* marching on, taking for itself all the tomorrows *you* had squandered. And don't get him started on Michigan. How did the unintelligible thing even end up on his dashboard? He'd have to remind Ivy to take it up to her room, or else it would remain in the back of his car for months.

. . .

"Do you realize how Snapchat *works*?" Dorothy asked him, her face lit up in the dark by her laptop. "That it just disappears? The photos they send each other? And that they can write captions on them? Then it all goes poof—like in five seconds it's gone. So there's no way of knowing what they're receiving, or putting out there, what images and messages they're being exposed to, there's no way to monitor any of it, because it vanishes . . ." She clicked on her trackpad. "Hey. Do you know about this?" He rolled toward her and grunted. "Uh-huh." With his mouth guard in, it wasn't easy to enunciate. She reached over to the nightstand and then dropped his neoprene eye mask onto his face, saying, "I think I'm going to be up for a little while." He heaved himself back onto his more comfortable side, the side with the good shoulder, and pulled the mask down over his eyes. Everything disappeared. There was something about being suddenly swaddled in darkness that made each of her clicks seem slightly louder than the one before, as if the source of the sound were coming, very slowly, closer.

. . .

The next morning, Dorothy returned from her run bearing a stack of newspapers in her arms, somewhat tentatively, like she was carrying someone else's baby. She dropped it heavily onto the island. "Since when do we subscribe to *The Guardian*?" she asked. "And *The New York Times*?" The dad looked up from his phone in confusion. He did recall making a few late-night donations to the NRDC and the Southern Poverty Law Center, but he'd forgotten all about the newspapers. "You know there's this thing called a digital subscription," she remarked as she opened the refrigerator. He moved out of her way. "That's what I did with *The Washington Post*," he said, remembering now. "Because they don't deliver outside the D.C. area."

"In a week this place is going to look like a hoarder's house," Dorothy predicted. "Piles of newspaper everywhere."

"I just think it's important to model," the dad said, looking meaningfully in the direction of the sofa. "Model where we get our information from."

He half expected his daughter's head to pop up like a groundhog's at the mention of "model." Kendall Jenner? Gigi Hadid? *No, not that kind of model*, he heard himself saying wearily over a laugh track.

Dorothy handed him a glass of juice. "Stop looking so pious," she said. "I agree with you."

. . .

New post: a hand holding a clear plastic Starbucks cup filled with a liquid the color of Pepto-Bismol. In it floated small chunks of something red.

. . .

"Do you think this is full of caffeine?" Dorothy asked, her screen tilted in his direction. Though they'd made a reservation, their table wasn't ready. They stood wedged into the little area by the door where umbrellas would have gone if it had been raining. "Who knows what they actually put in their drinks."

The door opened, the air was cold, and they squeezed closer together to let the new arrivals through.

"Well, she gets points for consistency, I'll give her that," Dorothy murmured as she continued thumbing her phone. "She's really thinking about her palette."

"Her pallet?" That was how he heard it, *pallet*, like where Joan of Arc would have slept.

"On her Instagram. It's pink. Her palette is a mix of light pink and hot pink."

He still didn't understand what she was talking about.

"With the occasional salmon accent thrown in."

He blinked angrily. Dorothy had downloaded the app only a week ago.

"What about the picture of Michelle Obama?" he asked. "She's not pink."

"Her dress is." His wife smiled at him.

At this point the hostess looked up from her station and signaled for them to approach. The noise of the restaurant rose up around them, and for a moment he felt enfolded by the warm lighting and the voices and the smell of food being thoughtfully prepared. But none of it gave him any pleasure.

As soon as they were seated, he ordered wine for them both and in a little bout of resentment told Dorothy that a pink palette struck him as depressingly clichéd. Ivy was just imitating what she saw other girls doing online. Carefully styled shots of doughnuts and videos of dissolving bath bombs. Groupthink, he said. She kept talking about her personal "style" and her "vibe" and her "aesthetic," but nothing about it was actually *hers*. The photo of her hand holding the pink drink from Starbucks? He'd seen practically the same image posted a hundred times before.

His wife reached out and touched the arm of a passing server. "Can we get a new fork, please?" Accidentally he had knocked his off the table.

. . .

"I know you don't like it when I talk about YouTubers, but can I tell you just this one thing? What makes Ashleigh Janine different from a lot of other YouTubers is that she's really honest with her fans. She'll come right out and say who's sponsoring her. She doesn't try to hide it or make it seem like it's just a coincidence that she uses Simple and Clinique. She'll say, 'I'm so excited to be working with these brands.' And also? She's grateful. She says all the time how blessed she is. Because she knows it's not usual for a twenty-three-year-old to be buying her first house. And have it be so big."

"She's buying a house?"

"With a pool."

"Wow," he said. "Her own pool."

"She's already moved in. Tomorrow she's going to Lowe's to buy houseplants."

"What's Simple?" He knew what Clinique was.

"It's a makeup remover. Like, cleansing facial wipes.

They don't use artificial perfumes or harsh chemicals, so it won't upset your skin."

"She bought a house by using cleansing wipes?"

"She has a lot of other sponsors, not just Simple. Plus she's writing a YA novel, so she gets money from that, too."

He didn't know how to continue the conversation. Accelerating, he made it through a yellow light.

"Dad?" his daughter said, after a minute or two. "When Ashleigh's book comes out, can I get it?"

He must have looked ill-disposed—or maybe he just looked ill—because then she said jovially, "Come on! It's *reading*."

But could it really be called reading? Did it actually count as a book? Or was it just something AMAZING. Something to be SO EXCITED about. To be SO GRATEFUL for. I hope you guys enjoyed it! I had so much fun doing it and if you want me to do more things like this, make sure to give it a big thumbs-up and comment down below. And don't forget to subscribe to my vlog channel—which just got, I can't believe it, two million subscribers!—because there you can see all the behind-the-scenes! So, yeah, thank you for watching and I love you guys so so so much—

In fact, would it be going too far to call it TREMENDOUS? Something INCREDIBLE. A massive story. And very complex. Made by some really incredible people. Of such incredible talent. It will be a big win, there's no question about it. And I can tell you why, because, number one, the enthusiasm. The enthusiasm for this, it is really tremendous—

Right before the impact, he heard his daughter gasp.

And, in the silence afterward, he felt her chest rising and falling rapidly against his outstretched arm.

. . .

New post: a bared collarbone with a seat-belt burn running diagonally across it. The welt shiny with ointment, and pink.

. . .

During the intermission of *The Nutcracker*, he was startled to see the physical therapist standing in line for the ladies' room. She was holding a potted orchid from Trader Joe's and wearing a velvet blazer. "You came!" he said, a little too loudly. He glanced around to see if maybe she had brought a date. She asked him, "Is this Ivy's mom?" and he remembered to introduce Dorothy, who promptly apologized for the length and overall tedium of the production. "But I'm enjoying it," the therapist protested. She complimented the girl who had danced Arabian Coffee and also the Chinese dragon dancers, who had succeeded, the dad admitted, in bringing a sort of unruly street energy to the show. "Ivy was wonderful," she said, and together he and Dorothy smiled. "Like you could really tell," he said.

She looked at him seriously. "I would know those legs anywhere. Overpronation of the feet, well-developed gastrocnemius. She was third from the back." The confidence with which she said it moved him. He wished he could say he knew anything that well. He thought of all the time she had spent working with his daughter deep in the forest of equipment: two times a week, for nearly three months. Not only a licensed professional but an expert in her field. And here she was, on her day off—

It was the therapist who was smiling now. "Don't look like that, Dave," she said. "It's not magic or anything. It's just my job." He began smiling, too, to show that he of course understood, but judging from the expression on her face, and on Dorothy's, it was very possible that his eyes were also leaking a little. The likelihood made him smile even more; that and the fact that—well, what do you know?—she did remember his name, after all.

. . .

A week after the performance, he came home late from work, and when he pulled the rental car into the driveway he saw his daughter sitting at the dining room table. She was framed photogenically by the room's picture window. For a moment, he felt the vise in his chest tightening—Why was she alone on a Friday night? Why hadn't Dorothy set up a sleepover for her? Why hadn't anyone invited her to their house?—but as he climbed out of the car he saw that she appeared unperturbed and in fact rather happy, or at least happily occupied. She had her earbuds in and was making Christmas cards, the supplies spread in a glittering swath across the table.

When she spotted him outside, she immediately yanked out her earbuds, pushed back her chair, and hurled herself against the picture window, landing with a soft thud. Her cheek lay smushed against the glass, her arms were splayed, and while she still needed one leg to stand on, she'd lifted the other and pressed its bent shape to the window. What in the world. He had no idea what she was expressing, or rehearsing—but the gesture was undoubtedly directed at him. Out in the darkness he gave her a thumbs-up, but her eyes were limply shut. Not a muscle moved. It was all very realistic.

Was he witnessing the magic of dance? Of—what was it called when she was little?—creative movement? Somehow she had managed to convey through her body precisely what he'd been feeling since November: not crushed, not flattened, but flung, as if from an obliterating blast, against a hard, exposing surface. Spread, embarrassed, suspended, without the strength to open his eyes and survey the damage. He put down his computer bag and drew closer to the window. He tapped lightly on the pane but she didn't flinch. Pressing his palm to hers, he wondered if she could feel his outline through the glass. He tried it with his other palm, and then his cheek. He raised and crooked his knee to match the angle of her leg. In sixth-grade theater class he'd had to do mirror games, but actually this was easier, because now he got to choose his partner. What was hard was balancing on one foot. When he started to wobble, her silent laughter made the whole window shake.

BEDTIME STORY

One long winter night, Ezra Washington's wife walks in on him telling their younger child stories from his rollerblading days. The room is as dark as a coal mine and his voice floats sonorously from somewhere in the vicinity of the trundle bed. He is remembering a time long before the child was born, a time when he was a poor graduate student living in New York City with nothing but his own body and mind for entertainment. Saturdays were spent in the narrow park that runs alongside the Hudson River, him blading up and down the path very fast as if his happiness depended on it.

"She was coming straight at me," he says. "To the right of me was the river. And to the left a pack of bicyclists. She was coming around the bend with a look of panic in her eyes."

From the doorway his wife wonders silently if he is speaking of her, the younger self who, on the three or four occasions on which she'd joined him, may have worn this expression.

"She was going fast, too?" their child asks in the dark.

"No, not at all, she was clearly a beginner. Which made

the situation that much more dangerous," Ezra says patiently. He then explains how he called out to her in the instant before they collided. *I've got you!* he cried to the inexperienced skater as he grasped her by the forearms and guided her down between his legs until her bottom gently touched ground. "By then she was laughing," he said. "That laugh you'd know anywhere."

His wife doesn't recall ever laughing while on Rollerblades. Her first wild thought is that all these years she's been wrong about herself. But then the child shifts in his bed and sets the comforter to rustling and casts the story in an entirely new light. "She's the one who plays the mom?" he asks. "With the big teeth and the long brown hair?"

"Well, I'd say it's more of a reddish brown. An auburn color. But yes, that's right," Ezra says to the child. "Julia Roberts."

"Julia Roberts went right between your legs," the child confirms.

"Yes, but don't repeat that," Ezra says. "Better to say we crashed into each other. Or that Julia Roberts crashed into me."

The child falls silent, as if committing this to memory.

Ezra adds, "It's not an exaggeration to say she was the biggest movie star in the world."

"Back then," the child clarifies.

Fine, his mother thinks, *back then*, all children by their nature sticklers, but in fact the poor kid has no idea. Never will he know the stunned sensation of emerging from the darkness of a matinee on Senior Skip Day, speechless at what they'd just seen: Julia Roberts as an adorable street-walker. It confounded the imagination. Whatever had possessed them to spend their day of mutiny in this ridiculous way? They would never forget it. A whole group of them milling about on the sidewalk outside the theater, boarding school students let loose on the world and now at a loss for what to do next, Ezra with his arm resting lightly across the shoulders of his girlfriend, Christina, his serious senior-year girlfriend Christina, and Christina looking shy and triumphant because already more than one person had said, *You know, you kind of look like her . . .*

Yes, she was there that day, witness to the spectacle of Ezra and Christina, and though she was sandwiched in the middle of the crowd, she saw them as if from a great distance, from a far, chilly point on the periphery. She kept half an eye on Ezra out of long habit, for she had done so, without quite wanting to, through all the weeks and months of high school that had come before, and maybe he had noticed: when he and Christina broke up after a run of graduation parties, it was she whom he called. He was miserable but talkative. One still had to pay for long distance in those days. On a Saturday morning in early October, he appeared on the steps of her freshman dorm, despite having enrolled at a college more than three hours away. By the time Ezra got into graduate school, they were an old couple, a familiar sight. She, too, had her tales of New York. The park he spoke of, and its hazardous paths—she once knew them well.

"Tell him," Ezra urges, his voice turned in her direction. It comes as a surprise: she thought she had gone unnoticed when she glided into the room, wearing socks.

"It's true," she says to their child. "Julia was huge. She was everywhere."

"And I bladed right into her," Ezra says with satisfaction, the splendor of the story holding all of them in its embrace. For a moment they absorb the fact of being together in the darkened bedroom, just the three of them, the older child probably off brushing his teeth somewhere. Ezra says to his wife, from the low edge of the bed, "You remember that day," in the sure-sounding voice she'd first liked in history class, and huskily she answers him, "Mm-hmm, I do," when in fact she has been quickly sifting through her brain only to find that she has no memory of it at all.

This is the second time today that her mind has failed her, but the first instance was so mild that it barely registered. In the late afternoon, drowsily driving the boys to their martial arts studio, she heard on the radio a story about the chain restaurant Medieval Times, where diners can watch live jousting tournaments while eating without the help of utensils. The big news was that the restaurant had decided to replace all of its resident kings with queens. Despite this change in leadership, the radio host remarked dryly, the servers at Medieval Times would still be referred to, going forward, as "wenches."

She perked right up at the sound of that friendly old word, which carried her instantly to the broken-backed couches and burnt-popcorn smell of their high school student center. For a brief spell there, *wench* had been the slur of choice—originating with the boys, one had to guess, but soon enough used in good-natured address from girl to girl. To her ears, it summoned not so much a barefoot slut with a tankard as the lanky, lacrosse-playing classmates of her youth, addled on weak hallucinogens and jam bands. The word filled her with sadness and warmth. But she couldn't for the life of her recall how to use it convincingly in a sentence. *Hey wench, good game today. Stop being such a wench and pass the popcorn. Bye, wench. Later, wench.* It all sounded wrong.

"Why are you talking to yourself?" her younger child asked from the back seat.

"I'm just trying to remember how to say something," she told him.

"In English?" he asked, sounding worried.

The problem, she sees now, is that in its heyday she never seized the chance to say the word herself. Nor was it ever said to her. So the failure wasn't of memory but of another sort. She hadn't shaped her lips around the word; it hadn't been lobbed fondly in her direction. Somehow the lacrosse players had known not to say it to her, or for that matter to any of the black girls, few as they were. For them, a tone of collegial respect had been specially reserved. So many pleasant exchanges, straightforward smiles! She might as well have been wearing a pantsuit during all those years. Yet dull Christina had been called a wench more times than could be counted. Along with a few humorous observations about the size of her mouth. Which would explain, wouldn't it, popular opinion regarding her resemblance to—

"Funny that she didn't have an entourage in tow," she says.

"Was she being followed by the paparazzi?" the child asks.

"Nope," Ezra answers serenely. "She was completely alone. Enjoying the day."

"Without even a bodyguard?" his wife asks in the dark.

"Not as far as I could see. But then again, I didn't see that it was Julia Roberts until I was looking down at her."

"Between your legs," the child says.

"I helped her back up to her feet and we each went on our way." Ezra is straightening out the comforter, by the sound of it. "I wasn't looking around for bodyguards. I wanted to get home as fast as I could and tell you."

"We didn't have cell phones," she explains.

"You were too poor," the child says soothingly.

She doesn't protest. The history of technology is too great an undertaking at this hour.

Also it's true: they lived on very little then. Home was a garden-level apartment in a neglected corner of an outer borough, its distance to the nearest subway stop the original inspiration behind the Rollerblades. From next door came the incoherent cries of an old man and the smell of decades' worth of fried meat. They kept the windows open in all seasons, because of both the smell and the furious radiators, controlled by some invisible hand.

A steel-legged café table with a laminate top was where they ate, worked, studied, and wrote thank-you notes. Despite the small checks that occasionally arrived in the mail from relatives living in less expensive places, Ezra still needed to have a part-time job while taking classes. He was descended from two generations of advanced-degree-holding black professionals who loved him unconditionally but regarded the project of "art school" with incredulity. *Graduate work in painting?* they'd repeat, as if maybe they had misunderstood. As for her, she'd inherited her parents' immigrant terror of nonfamilial debt, and so had yet to apply for even a credit card, much less to a graduate program. They were extortionists preying on directionless people in their mid-to-late twenties, and she wasn't interested. She liked the magic of direct deposit and also the green-bordered Social Security statement that would appear every few years, telling her just how much she had earned so far in her working life. After moving to New York, she promptly found employment, with benefits, in the alumni relations office at Ezra's school. Her parents approved of the job but seemed undecided, even after all this time, about Ezra. When she watched television with them, the handsomeness of a young actor might make her mother pensive. "You have to be careful with a man who's better-looking than you," she'd been heard to say, to a character onscreen.

Every day his girlfriend set off for the university uncomplainingly, but Ezra wanted to be on campus no more than what was already required. Instead he got a job at a gym. He had to wear an orange polo shirt with the gym's logo stitched over his left pectoral. Standing at a counter, he scanned members' ID cards as they entered and then checked on the computer to make sure that their payments were up to date. This was how he first learned her name, Meg Sand. He was familiar with her name long before he noticed her looking at him from the lat machine. Or gazing, maybe. It was hard to tell the nature of the look from across the expanse of equipment, under the gym's flattening fluorescent light. Either way she had her pale eyes fixed on him, and every once in a while, in the middle of a set, she gave him an effortful smile. The amount of weight she was lifting, he saw, was significant. An immense iron stack rose up slowly behind her like an omen.

"Thanks," she said, as she turned in her towel.

"Why, hello," he said jokingly, leaning forward on the counter.

Meg Sand wore a stretchy top that matched her reflective leggings, new sneakers, and a full face of makeup. The makeup wasn't loud; she looked like a girl who had moved to the city from upstate and, upon the shock of arrival, severely trained herself in how to do things nicely. She clutched a rather elegant brown purse. Her voice was deeper than he'd expected and when she spoke to him she sounded unnatural, as if she were a grown-up trying to be pals with a kid. Did he also work out here? Or just work? She laughed lamely at herself. Yet Meg Sand was, according to the computer, practically the same age as him. Not even a full year older. It was her hair, he realized: she wore it short and gently teased, in a mature little pouf, a style chosen, he saw with a pang, to conceal the fact that it was thinning.

Quickly enough he developed the trick of not letting his eyes drift above her forehead. Sitting at the Polish restaurant around the corner from the gym, he would watch her tuck into a plate of cherry blintzes and finish off a big glass of ice water. She seemed to take undue pride in not being the type of gym-goer who only ate healthy. The booth's seats were sticky and made funny sounds whenever he adjusted himself, which he did often, sucking listlessly at a fountain soda and describing what had happened that week in crit. She would listen with a stolid expression and barely move. To his surprise, she did not share an upsetting story straightaway, as white girls who liked him were in the habit of doing, a story told slowly, as if with reluctance, but always aired fully by the time they were making out. Bulimia and bad parents. Depression. Social pressures, double standards, a sister who had been hospitalized. All offered unconsciously, he guessed, in a nervous spirit of redress. Yet Meg Sand rarely said anything about herself. And *girl*, in her case, didn't exactly fit.

Without making a big fuss, she'd pay the bill for both of them. Together they would walk to his subway station and after giving her a brisk hug he'd jog downstairs into the clatter and the heat, feeling light of heart. Nothing was going on. Nothing was going on! He sailed into the basement apartment, pulled off his orange polo shirt, and made love under the open window to his beautiful girlfriend. He planned, any day now, to propose to her. But not on his knees: they already spent enough time as it was practically underground. Instead he imagined, absurdly, a wide empty field, where he would toss the glittering ring in the air and she would catch it with her outstretched hands.

It was not only his heart that felt newly light. His legs on the long walk to the subway, his hand as it moved across a thick sheet of paper. His advisor's caustic sense of humor, which had made him insecure at the start of the semester, was now a source of amusement and private laughter. The gym regulars no longer greeted him as "Man" or "Dude" but by his real name. *Hey, Ezra, what's up.* Rearranging the free weights took almost no effort at all. He felt agile and clearheaded. His skin looked good. Out of the depths of her boxy brown purse, Meg Sand produced little tubes and flasks of extravagant ointments made by companies he'd never heard of before. She worked in a large department store on the housewares floor, but she claimed to have friends at all the cosmetic counters, and these were samples, she said. They were free.

From inside the humid broom closet they called their bathroom came his girlfriend's gentle voice. "I have to say these look regular-sized to me," she said clearly. He had emptied a shelf in the medicine cabinet so he could create a display. The little flasks were elegant, and he had nothing to hide. Only a month before, the three of them had gone to the movies and watched a terrible action thriller. His idea, both the movie and their meeting each other. The whole thing had come together in such a casual way as to feel practically spontaneous.

His girlfriend had met them at the theater. She was coming straight from work, from an alumni networking event that she had helped organize, and as she approached them he could tell that one of her high heels had started to hurt. He could also tell that she immediately took in the problem of Meg Sand's hair. Her whole face relaxed. The job in retail, the degree from SUNY Potsdam, now the hair: there truly was no cause for alarm. Meg Sand stumbled backward slightly as his girlfriend went in for a hug. Oh, she was a ruthless snob, as only the recently respectable can be. Before she even said hello, he knew that she would speak to Meg in the silvery, childlike voice she used when communicating with maintenance staff or bus drivers, as if making her voice smaller might somehow diminish the existential distance between them.

Once the movie was over, they stood outside on the street, shivering. He didn't suggest that they go get a coffee somewhere. His girlfriend had slipped off her shoes in the theater and when the credits started to roll, had a difficult time getting them back on again. Her blouse was softly askew, the long day had loosened her hair, and he wanted to take her home and into bed.

But she persisted in being gracious. "Did you enjoy it?" she asked Meg Sand, who paused, shot a furtive look at the movie poster, and then seemed to remember the risk-free response she had prepared for these occasions. "It wasn't what I was expecting," she said slowly. She gave one of her close-lipped, knowing smiles: a precaution she used all the time, he'd noticed, a smile showing that whatever the joke at hand might be, she was in on it.

"Me neither!" his girlfriend replied. "A lot more blood than I signed up for. And all that gurgling when people died. It was very graphic. Or is that more sound design? They didn't leave anything to the imagination, did they. Her knife skills were—amazing."

Meg brightened a bit. "Amazing. Yes. I loved the fight sequences. She was so fierce. I think she must have trained for a long time to play the part. I read somewhere that she did most of the stunt work herself."

"Well, I believe it," his girlfriend said. "The action looked very real."

"I must have read that in the *Times*," Meg went on. "Yes, that must have been where I read it. In last weekend's Arts section."

"Oh! Did you see that piece about Merce Cunningham and the dog?"

Meg shook her head mutely.

"It was funny." His girlfriend smiled at Meg with almost professional kindness. Then she tilted her head and narrowed her eyes. "You know, with that jacket on, you kind of look like—" She said the forgettable name of the actress. "Especially the whole section when she's in Budapest. I'm not imagining it."

He didn't see the resemblance himself. He told them flatly that he thought the movie was garbage. "You thought so, too," he said to his girlfriend as they rode the subway back to their outer borough. She shrugged sleepily. "I didn't want to be judgmental," she murmured, placing her head on his shoulder. By the time they reached their stop, she was dead to the world. He had to guide her up the stairs and through the empty streets like a parent steering a child toward bed.

As the end of winter dragged on, Meg Sand wore the jacket more often than not. Was it coincidence that she also bought a pair of tall, zippered boots similar to the ones worn by the female assassin? "I used my employee discount," she said apologetically from her side of the booth. He'd had to ask for more hours at the gym, in order to recover from the reckless amount he'd spent on a new computer. Also, his girlfriend was preparing to take an unpaid leave from her job at the alumni office; she'd already used up all her vacation days by the time they found out about her mother's breast cancer. At first she had wept uncontrollably, but then she became very quiet and matter-of-fact, and started researching airfares. It was Stage II, they caught it early, she wouldn't even need chemo. A lumpectomy, not a mastectomy. These facts he repeated to Meg Sand in their corner of the Polish restaurant, as if to reassure himself. Nothing had prepared him for the secondhand jitters he was feeling. The container ship that had looked toylike on the horizon was now, upon making its way into port, revealing its true dimensions. Since the scheduling of the surgery, he'd been having trouble falling asleep, and though Meg ordered him a Coke, he hardly touched it.

With his girlfriend gone, he was thankful for the company of his new computer, which was faster than his old one to an incredible degree. The enormous monitor, the powerful processor, the highly sensitive keyboard—all necessary now that he had decided to expand his practice into video. The overall lack of light in the basement apartment was proving to be a plus. He was hypnotized by the way that editing could turn the sloppy footage he'd shot at school into something rich with possible meaning. A sudden cut to black, the amplification of ambient sound. Hours melted away without his realizing it. The first weekend he spent alone, he managed to get groceries and do his laundry, but the second weekend he didn't leave the apartment at all. When the telephone rang, he had no sense of whether it was this day or the next, and as he answered, confused, his heart inexplicably racing, the unbearable thought that occurred to him was: She's dead.

"Ezra? I'm sorry to bother you." The deep, uninflected voice of Meg Sand was on the other end. He was briefly even more confused, and then strangely comforted that it was only her. "I know I shouldn't be calling this late. I tried calling two other people before I called you."

"Is it late?" he asked. "I don't even know what time it is."

"It's 11:47," she replied. "It's almost midnight."

As she was speaking, he saw that the time had been right

in front of him all along, tucked away in a corner of his vast computer screen. "Look at that," he said aloud. Then he realized: "I think the last meal I ate was breakfast."

"I'm sorry," Meg said again, and fell silent before announcing, "But I've been robbed."

He flew across the city in the back of a Lincoln Town Car whose shocks seemed in need of immediate replacement. The traffic lights turned green one after the other, benevolently synchronized, as if wishing him Godspeed as he drew ever closer to Meg's apartment. He didn't know what he would find there. A jimmied lock, a gaping window, stuff spilling out of drawers, strewn across the floor, or . . . ? Darkened blocks scrolled past the smudged glass. With a sense of deliverance he understood that, whatever crisis he encountered, he'd be able to help. And if it turned out that in the end he couldn't— well, she was just a friend from the gym. Teeth rattling, he hurtled forward, at once weightless and full of purpose.

Her address was on York Avenue, which despite its Manhattan zip code appeared to be even more desolate and remote than where he lived. The car jerked to a stop in front of her building; he looked up at its expanse of monotonous midcentury brick and felt depressed for her. She was waiting in the lobby, dressed in her jacket and boots. He almost didn't notice the doorman sitting wordlessly at his station but then found himself wondering about him as they rose upward in the elevator. On the seventh floor, she led him down a carpeted corridor to her apartment door, which she unlocked with trembling hands. It swung open onto a single room that contained her entire life: stove, bed, clothes rack, television, all laid out plainly before him. On the wall hung a poster-size reproduction of a black-and-white photo of the Flatiron Building, framed. The bed was piled high with expensive-looking pillows of different shapes and sizes that she must have acquired through her job. She went to the little stove and started boiling water—not in a teakettle but in a saucepan.

"I hope you like chamomile," she said. "It's all I have."

He couldn't find an obvious place where he was meant to sit. He couldn't figure out what had been stolen. The room had a slightly tousled look but seemed otherwise intact.

"How did they get in?"

She turned from the stove and looked at him uncomprehendingly.

"The—robbers." He corrected himself. "Intruders." But maybe it had been someone working solo. "Intruder," he said, finally.

She blinked once, then twice, as if trying to bring him into focus. "It happened on the subway," she said. "Is that what you mean?"

"I don't mean anything. You're the one who said you were robbed." He glared at the apartment around him, searching for signs of entry. "And I said that I would come right over. Which I did."

"Thank you," Meg said. "Thank you for coming over. You didn't have to. I feel bad that it's so late."

"I don't care what time it is. I'm just not understanding what you—"

"It happened on the subway," she repeated. "It must have happened when I was on my way home from work.

Because then I got back and took a shower and ordered Thai and when I went to pay the delivery guy I reached into my bag and it wasn't there."

"Your wallet?"

"Yes. It was gone. The last time I had it was when I pulled out a token."

"You think someone stole it on the subway," he said dully. "Hours ago. Like a pickpocket."

"Yes," she answered solemnly, and handed him his cup of tea. "I do."

Before taking the cup, he put down his backpack, heavy with the hammer and nails he had brought. The tea smelled medicinal and was too hot to drink. He had paid thirty-eight dollars for the car service, with tip. He was overcome by the sudden, profound tiredness that comes right after a stupid expenditure of energy. Meg was now sitting on the edge of her bed, still wearing her jacket, as if she, too, were a guest. Without asking, he sank down beside her and placed his cup on the floor. He was too exhausted even to be angry anymore.

"So," he said. "This is your place."

"Welcome," she said, and with a little sigh rested her fragile head of hair on his shoulder. "I'm glad you're here."

At least that's how Ezra's wife has imagined it, their unpromising start. Some details, such as the poster of the Flatiron Building and the mound of fancy pillows, she is familiar with from the video; some—the lat machine, the good purse, the booths at the Polish restaurant—she knows firsthand; the rest are the result of inference and extrapolation. It is rare for her to think at all of Meg Sand anymore, but the mention of Julia Roberts there in the dark has brought her back.

When Ezra recalls his years in graduate school, his memory has occasionally confused or conflated the two of them—her and Meg. To be fair, the instances have been very few. In one case, she had to remind him that they didn't watch the Knicks lose to the Spurs in the finals; she was in Florida with her parents. Also, she can say with certainty that she's never discovered a mouse behind the toaster oven. Or been pickpocketed on the subway. She wonders if the same could be true of the rollerblading event. She believes that it was an experience he enthusiastically recounted at the time, just not to her.

Yet her memory is not without its own shortcomings. She cannot remember, for example, Meg Sand's last name. Sand is just something she's made up as a placeholder. Whatever the real name is, she thinks, it must be so ordinary, so unremarkable, as to be mind-numbing in the most literal sense. For a while she thought it might have been Whitman, until realizing that that was the name of the CEO who had run unsuccessfully for governor of California. Because she can't remember Meg Sand's real name, she hasn't been able to repeat it to herself and she hasn't been able to look her up online.

But she doubts that she would ever type Meg's name into a search box, even if she could. Her curiosity is nil. There's nothing more she wants to know. For the nearly twenty years that she's had the video in her possession, not once has she felt the faintest need to watch it again. The first time was enough, and even then she didn't watch it all the way through. Very clearly she remembers how surprised she was that she could operate the playback function on the camera in the first place. She'd never used the camera before or been interested in how it worked. But there was something about the way it was resting beneath Ezra's desk, balanced casually on top of the paper shredder, its little screen popped open, that made her stop.

She put down the box she was carrying. Inside, still in its protective wrapping, was a five-piece place setting of the wedding china that Ezra's aunts had gently insisted they register for. There was no room or use for china in their basement apartment. With ceremonial care she had been stacking the boxes in the corner of the bedroom not already taken up by Ezra's massive computer. Though he had gallantly carried her over the threshold, marriage had done little to change their abode other than to make it feel smaller and darker. When she put down the china, the last to arrive, her hands were shaking. This is another detail she recalls with perfect clarity: her hands shaking even before she picked up the camera and turned it on.

A bed piled with tasseled pillows; a framed black-and-white poster, only a corner of which appears in the shot; a long white body, naked except for a pair of knee-high gladiator sandals. The soles of the sandals as flat and beige as pancakes.

And then from offscreen his voice, the voice that she had first heard in history class, telling the body what he'd like it to do.

She couldn't hit the square of the stop button quickly enough. Straightaway she ejected the cassette, which was smaller than a tin of breath mints. She wandered back and forth the length of the apartment, holding it carefully in the palm of her hand. She thought about stuffing it down to the bottom of the garbage can, or wrapping it in layers of newspaper and tossing it in a dumpster, or dropping it down the echoing trash chute at work. She also thought about cracking open the plastic shell and plucking out the two black reels inside and melting them over the stove—then wondered about the strands of videotape she sometimes saw tangled in the branches of the borough's trees. How did they end up there? Meanwhile, a cold little part of her counseled prudence: keep it safe. At which she recoiled: it would poison her. After several minutes of this, she called Ezra at the gym to say that she was leaving him. The word *divorce* she avoided, not wanting to sound operatic. By the time he arrived home, she had already changed her mind ten or eleven times as to what she needed to do.

He was breathing very hard. He had run the entire way from the distant subway stop. On his sweating face was the naked look of fear that comes with having loved someone for a long time. "You're still here," he panted. The look on his face summoned out of her chaotic feelings the lifelong habit of pragmatism, which caused her to say with formality, "She is not to see or contact us ever again," a message that she repeated a few days later when Meg Sand called the apartment, and she was startled to hear herself speak not in her lilting telephone voice but in an unfamiliar and shaky middle register that seemed to emanate directly from her chest. She hung up the receiver before the person on the other end could respond. Her mind was still changing rapidly, hourly. The only thing she knew for certain was that the video had become hers in some permanent, irrefutable way. She buried the cassette in the deep pocket of a shearling coat she no longer wore but that still hung thickly at the back of the closet, and so it remained there undisturbed for many years and through several moves, until the technology that it required had all but disappeared.

Could the nature of the video be interpreted in a different way? The therapist at the university health center had asked her this question. Your husband is studying art, she said, double-checking the open folder in her lap. Was there anything—the therapist searched for a word—*artistic* about what you saw?

Grimly, she said no. They had been over this before. Therapy was turning out to be deserving of the suspicion in which she had always held it, but under her benefits plan the first six sessions were free. The truth is, she was too shy to explain to the therapist why she had instantly recognized the sort of video she was watching. Just as she was too shy to keep her eyes open while making them. Darkness was essential, she couldn't explain; darkness was key.

The darkness created when he turned on the camera and she closed her eyes—was it the same element that she's standing in now, listening to him say good night to their child? She likes to think that it is, the dark being the only thing large, comfortable, and cluttered enough to contain all the various bits and pieces of their life together. So many years between them, and from where exactly does one begin to count? The first day of ninth grade, or the short, rainy summer after graduation? The moment they signed a lease and became residents of the basement apartment? There is no single starting point, only the density and shapelessness of experience held in common, the meals prepared and eaten, the assorted haircuts and injuries, elations and malaises, car leases and checking accounts, friends made, trips taken, a pregnancy that failed and two that didn't. She remembers: the shock of a baby's cold mouth on her nipple after he spat out an ice pop and chose her breast instead. He remembers: her shout of laughter. Now their younger child kicks experimentally at the comforter, unwilling to go to sleep, while the older one makes his way up the stairs, halting at irregular intervals, absorbed no doubt by the game in his hand, lighting his face from below as he moves slowly toward them.

"Pick up the pace, kid." Ezra casts his voice toward the door. "We're all waiting."

It is the same voice, and also the same darkness: the darkness out of which this voice once floated, low-pitched and warm, patiently unfolding and finding her on the bed, the bed seeming to lift imperceptibly off the floor, set aloft yet lightly tethered, his voice telling her what he saw, what he liked, the things he wished to see more of. At the sound of his voice, she relaxed into the pleasure of being instructed, and then more deeply into the pleasure of being seen, and running beneath it all was a bright, nearly invisible current of thankfulness. To be called such things. In words far worse, or far better, than whatever had been said in high school. Tipping back her head and closing her eyes, she felt capable of doing anything he asked. She saw pictures: a bar of sunlight flaring on a mirror; the square, golden windows of a long motel at night. His steady voice spoke to her in the dark. "Wider," he said, and she opened farther than she had thought possible.